A Rainbow
Murder Mystery

Praise for Murder at Stonehenge—

Murder at Stonehenge is brilliant, imaginative, and suspenseful, a superb sequel to *Murder on Easter Island*. Gary D. Conrad is a gifted storyteller who delights in the unexpected and unusual. A page turner.

—Carolyn Hart, author of the Bailey Ruth series

If the legendary Carl Jung had turned out to be a murder-mystery writer instead of a world-famous psychiatrist and expert in alchemy and mythology, this is the thriller he would have written. *Murder at Stonehenge* is an exciting romp through archaeology, mythology, history, and plain ol' good and evil. Buckle up and plunge in!

—Larry Dossey, MD, author of *One Mind: How Our Individual Mind Is Part of a Greater Consciousness and Why It Matters*

Murder at Stonehenge is a rollicking mystery that skillfully moves the reader to and from the spiritual, the secular, the mystical and the bizarre. Gary Conrad builds the tension from chapter to chapter to astonishing levels; I found myself unable to turn the pages fast enough. If you want to know more about the history of Stonehenge and at the same time enjoy a wild and unpredictable mystery, this is a book for you.

—Andrew Weil, MD, author of *Spontaneous Happiness* and *Healthy Aging*

Daniel Fishinghawk takes on another seemingly insolvable case, this time at the site of one of the world's most enduring mysteries. Gary Conrad constructs his investigation with attention to the environment and history. A rare mystery with a spiritual dimension.

—William Bernhardt, author of *Justice Returns*

In *Murder at Stonehenge*, Conrad demonstrates once again his skill at weaving a compelling story. His research is thorough. His insights are wise. His characters live and love. And his readers will come to know what they've always suspected about their own lives, that the past and present are inextricably bound.

—Sheldon Russell, author of *The Bridge Troll Murders*

Everyone who enjoyed reading *Murder on Easter Island* will be delighted to read *Murder at Stonehenge*. With these two engaging novels Gary Conrad dares to leap into the most magical of places, combining history, imagination, exotic locations and suspense.

—Joan Korenblit, Respect Diversity Foundation

Science and spirituality, intuition and deduction, old and new worlds, time travel and cross-cultural exchanges — Gary Conrad's writing is sure to enthrall readers of mysteries everywhere — especially those committed to sacrificial love, perhaps the ultimate mystery.

—Ken Hada, author of *Bring an Extry Mule* and *Persimmon Sunday*

In the further adventures of Hawk and his time-travelling wife Mahina, Gary Conrad offers another cracking murder mystery romp, combining mythology and mysticism . . . With parallel narratives set on Rapanui and in England, there is double the action and intrigue as Hawk and Mahina struggle against an evil spiritual force and the equally dangerous forces of human greed and violence. There are also elements of humour as Hawk engages with English eccentricities, including the use of language. No doubt something Conrad encountered himself during his fieldwork research to Stonehenge and other ancient sites in the United Kingdom.

—Dr. Roy Smith, Course Leader,
MA International Development,
Nottingham Trent University, UK

Journeying from Easter Island to darkest rural England and the monolithic circle of Stonehenge, Gary Conrad has created a new murder mystery that expertly captures the wonders of the ancient world.

—Professor Ian Conrich (University of Vienna)

Murder at STONEHENGE

GARY D. CONRAD

Rainbow Books, Inc.
FLORIDA

Murder at Stonehenge: A Daniel "Hawk" Fishinghawk Mystery © 2019 by Gary D. Conrad

Hardcover ISBN: 978-1-56825-195-0
Softcover ISBN: 978-1-56825-196-7
EPUB ISBN: 978-1-56825-197-4

Cover image from iStockPhoto.
Author photo by Sheridan Conrad.

Published by:
Rainbow Books, Inc.
P. O. Box 430, Highland City, FL, 33846-0430
Telephone: (863) 648-4420 • RBIbooks@aol.com • RainbowBooksInc.com

Author's Website:
GaryDConrad.com

Individuals' Orders:
Amazon.com • AllBookStores.com • BN.com • BookCH.com

This is a work of fiction. Any resemblance of characters to individuals living or dead is coincidental.

Seekers of the Healing Energy by Mary Coddington, published by Inner Traditions International and Bear & Company © 1978, 1990. All rights reserved. http://www.InnerTraditions.com Reprinted with permission of publisher.

All rights reserved. No part of this book may be reproduced or transmitted in any form or by any means, electronic or mechanical (except as follows for photocopying for review purposes). Permission for photocopying can be obtained for internal or personal use, the internal or personal use of specific clients, and for educational use, by paying the appropriate fee to: Copyright Clearance Center, 222 Rosewood Dr., Danvers, MA, 01923, USA

Written, produced and printed in the United States of America.

To Sheridan
My wife, best friend and inspiration
My companion
Through the journey of life

Murder at STONEHENGE

Prelude One

The most important day of her life had arrived.

Tiare Rapu, the last shaman of the Rapanui, sat quietly on the rocky floor of the seaside cave, Ana Kai Tangata, which lay at ocean level, just southwest of the Easter Island city of Hanga Roa. She watched quietly as turbulent ocean waves ten feet high crashed onto the volcanic rocks at the mouth of the cave, producing showers of sea spray and the warm, comforting aroma of salty air. The rolling pattern of the breakers created a naturally rhythmic sound, perfect for deep meditation, which she and her people called dreaming.

Ana Kai Tangata, translated literally into cave-eat-man, was a mysterious location where legend said cannibalism had occurred in the past. Most archaeologists had officially stated there was no evidence of such a barbaric practice on Easter Island; but, as a shaman, Tiari was also keeper of the island's oral prehistory, so she knew better. Cannibalism was indigenous in Polynesia, and Easter Island—Rapa Nui to the natives—was no exception.

She glanced up to the ceiling of the cave, high above her, and studied the old red, black and white paintings of manutara birds in flight. *No doubt created in association with past Birdman competitions,* she thought, *from times long past.* Daniel, her new friend from the States, had endured the treacherous, coming-of-age event for young native men after his exploration of another of Rapa Nui's mysterious and enchanted caves landed him in ancient Rapa Nui.

Tiare had long felt out of balance, though, because at ninety-five years of age, she had yet to accomplish one of the most important goals for a shaman, and the responsibility weighed heavily upon her. She shuddered in concern as she realized, once again, that she had yet to choose a successor.

The Rapanui will need a shaman. The thought was ever present in her mind. *Even in modern times—especially in modern times. Daniel's brush with evil had proven that.* She felt well, however, and guessed her death was not imminent but knew the veil between living and dying was as thin as parchment paper for someone her age. She had long sought to dream in this cave because it was important to prepare for her own death by choosing a replacement, and the time to do so was now.

No longer can I wait.

The occasion was truly momentous, and most of the time, she dreamed by herself, but today, she decided to enlist the wisdom of one who had been her guide throughout her life: the sea turtle, *honu* in the Rapanui tongue. Tiare had been taught that shamans worldwide, from time immemorial, connected with what some preferred to call power animals. Her Polynesian ancestors saw animals as god-like creatures that possessed an understanding of Nature and her interactions that mere humans would have a difficult time comprehending. Even as a modern shaman, Tiare also looked to animal spirits as mentors and allies through all of the enigmas that life presented, and there were many.

Tiare sadly remembered why sea turtle visits had become so rare to Rapa Nui. In times past, the flesh of the sea turtle was an important source of food, and stone towers, called *tupas*, built for watching the stars, were constructed along the shoreline to predict when the turtles would visit the island. Unfortunately, due to the starvation that faced her ancestors, most that came ashore were eaten, and with time, their visits to the island diminished.

Tiare sighed as she thought back to her introduction to her sea turtle friend. She was but a scrawny, dark-eyed girl of twelve, when one warm morning, her shaman father, Tuki Vaka, who was tall and muscular with shoulder-length black hair, invited her to accompany him to the deep ocean in his makeshift canoe, hoping to catch some fish for their noontime meal.

The ocean was rough that day, and after they rowed out for about an hour, a rogue, cresting wave hit their canoe and sent Tiare and her father flying into the water. Tuki Vaka quickly resurfaced and grabbed the side of the overturned vessel, but his darling Tiare was nowhere to be seen. He yelled her name and searched for her, diving over and over again into the frothy water. Despite his shaman training, which had taught him to control his emotions, fear and panic captured his usually serene mind. Seconds turned to minutes, and each time he resurfaced, he screamed her name in agony before he plunged back as deeply as he could into the choppy sea, searching frantically.

After far too long for comfort, Tiare's father grasped the side of the canoe to catch his breath. As he spun around in his frenzy, he saw something approach from the distance.

What is it? He squinted to help make it out.

Even though he was a shaman and had learned to expect the unusual, he was astonished to realize it was Tiare moving toward him—on the back of the largest sea turtle he had ever seen. Tuki Vaka managed to flip the canoe upright, just as the sea turtle paused in front of him, its multicolored shell glowing in the bright Rapa Nui sun. He gently lifted an unconscious Tiare, her left arm broken and angulated, over the side and into the canoe.

Her father placed his right hand on the turtle's back and reverently whispered, "Thank you, Honu, oh great one."

The sea turtle's wise gaze, full of wisdom, fell on Tuki Vaka for a moment, then it slowly disappeared into the now-calm water. Tuki Vaka knew, at that moment, that Tiare was to be a shaman, and he promised himself, once her arm was mended, he would begin her training in earnest.

Tiare didn't have a memory of the sea turtle or her ride on its back. All she remembered, after being violently propelled from the canoe, was floating in an ocean of bliss, feeling safe, and knowing, deep inside, the love she now inexplicably felt would be with her forever. Later, after her father had related the story to her, she knew the love had come from her new friend, the sea turtle—Honu. So, whenever she was in great need, she called Honu's name, as she prepared to do now.

Tiare closed her eyes and pulled her consciousness deep inside her being. When her breath became shallow and nearly imperceptible, she silently said to herself:

Honu . . . Honu . . . Honu.

She continued the calls from her heart repeatedly, powerfully and with focused intent:

Honu... Honu... Honu.

Suddenly, Tiare felt bathed in love, the same love she experienced when she first met the sea turtle, and a sudden shimmering light radiated from her forehead. She transformed into a scintillating being of light, in the shape of a twelve-year-old girl, effortlessly floating in a sparkling, crystal-clear sea that teemed with swarms of brightly colored ocean fish.

Honu serenely drifted in front of her, head raised, eyes focused on Tiare.

Tiare said lovingly, in Rapanui, "Honu, you have once again come to me."

Of course, my child. Have I ever not responded to your bidding?

"Never," Tiare confirmed, with strength in her voice. "I now have a most important and urgent question for you, one I should have asked long ago."

Honu's words were low and soft as they filled Tiare's mind: *This is not a question you could have asked before now.*

"I don't understand."

When you know the answer, you will.

"Then," Tiare asked, "whom should I choose to be my shaman successor?"

You already know.

"What do you mean?" Her breath quickened.

You are a wise shaman, Honu calmly imparted to her, *wiser than any I have ever known through the eons. The answer already exists inside you.*

Tiare spread her arms open and pleaded, "Please... help me."

Very well, then. I will pose a riddle. Answer it, and you will know. Are you ready?

"I am."

Honu silently spoke:

> *The one you seek*
> *Was once a distant memory*
> *Yet now she lives*
> *Bringing the seeds of the ancient past*
> *And the wisdom of the ages*
> *Into the now*
> *The lineage continues*

Honu asked, *Do you now understand?*

"I do. Thank you, my friend."

Honu added, *I give you my knowledge freely and with joy. But beware—I see great danger approaching for you and your chosen apprentice.*

"What kind of danger?"

That, you must discover for yourself. Honu paused for a moment. *You should be aware that evil is close—closer than you could possibly imagine.*

"But—"

The vision ended abruptly, and Tiare once again became aware of sitting in the cave, concerned and deeply missing the ecstatic love of the vision.

She sighed, tried to brush away her worries and continued to listen to her breath. Recalling Honu's warning, Tiare probed the depths of the cave with her shaman mind. In a flash, she became aware of a murky, sinister presence, one that abruptly disappeared.

Tiare shrugged her shoulders and once again tried to focus on the comfort of Honu's love, but she found herself unable to do so. Her brief visionary glimpse had revealed that the evil was powerful, one she must prepare for.

Tiare looked inside herself and knew she had the spiritual resources to deal with the presence. *But what if that somehow changed?*

Tiare breathed deeply into her concerns and watched as they slowly dissipated.

Prelude Two

Penny Pumpernickel stood on a rolling library ladder and busily feather dusted the upper shelves of her shop, Teas of the World, located on Catherine Street in downtown Salisbury, England. Closing time was approaching, and she wanted the store to be clean and shipshape before she locked the doors.

Her Black Forest cuckoo clock announced six p.m., and, realizing that no one remained in the store, she stepped down from the ladder. She looked out the window, saw the streets were empty, clicked the front door shut and secured it with a dead bolt. She dutifully flipped the *Open* sign to *Closed*, blew out her clove-scented candle, sat in an antique oak chair by the front door and admired her wares.

How long have I been at this now? Nineteen years?

She was proud to be widely considered a connoisseur of teas, and she loved sharing the minutest details about the varieties with her customers. She sighed contentedly.

She remembered with satisfaction her special Tasty Days promotions, which allowed her patrons to come in and "enjoy a few samples from a choice array of teas for half price." Penny was especially fond of promoting the organic varieties, all the rage, but her long-standing favorite was pu-erh. "A fermented, dark tea produced in the Yunnan province of China." She enjoyed describing to customers how pu-erh tea was aged in underground rooms or caves, and the longer it matured, the better it got. Some were allowed to age for years, she would tell them, and, like fine wines, were unbelievably expensive—but not on Tasty Days.

The customers hung on my every word. She closed her eyes and smirked. *And they bought and they bought.*

It was going to be difficult for her loyal clients to accept that, in just a few short months, she would be leaving her shop. Earlier in the week, she had placed a sign in the front window that announced:

> Dearest Customers,
>
> In the coming months,
> Teas of the World will be operated
> by new proprietors, a group from London.
> Thank You for Your Patronage.
>
> Fondly, Penny Pumpernickel, Proprietor

Penny knew her patrons were worried that the store would lose the personality that only a sole proprietor could give. They had told her as much and had begged her not to go. Some boldly asked what she had planned after the sale, and she would only shrug a shoulder, give them a wink.

If they only knew what I was truly about . . . my brilliant secrets. Secrets I've kept to myself for all of these years. Secrets that cannot, under any circumstances, be shared. She had been so very careful not to.

The secrets originated some twenty years ago, when she, along with a select, secret group of intellectuals from other countries, began a move to Salisbury to join forces with a local team. Not all at once, of course; they didn't want to arouse suspicion. So they had unanimously agreed that their migration was to be spread over a five year period. Penny found their purpose titillating: research in a hidden location on the outskirts of town—research that could potentially lead to enormous wealth for everyone involved.

Penny's hands involuntarily rubbed together at the very thought of it. And she thought of it at the end of every day.

She had dragged her school teacher husband, Duncan, to Salisbury from Edinburgh, Scotland under the pretense of opening this very tea shop. Of course, she did just that, but little did Duncan know that her business-to-be—the tea shop—was a sham with a deeper, darker purpose, one she could never share with him.

After ten years of barely seeing his wife because she worked in her shop during the day and mysteriously disappeared most evenings, Mr. Pumpernickel threw up his hands in frustration and divorced her.

Penny snickered as she thought about it: *I never loved him anyway.* He had ballooned to over three hundred pounds, and she thought he smelled like the ass end of a donkey lying in a bed of wet, soggy manure.

He was disgusting, she almost said aloud. *Why did he never take a shower?*

There was nothing to keep them together; they had no children, and she was sick of hearing his snoring night after night, in spite of her wearing ear plugs, taking sleeping pills, and his using a CPAP machine.

I'm glad we divorced, more money for me. No sharing with that morbidly obese slob who used to be my husband.

She inventoried the events of the past twenty years, which she thought had been most interesting. But one thing had stalled the plan: Though the group was composed of some of the brightest minds in the world, they had been repeatedly unsuccessful in bringing their experiment to fruition. They had tried everything, or so they thought.

Desperation led to many risky trials, which eventually resulted in two of their group going completely mad. Ian Johansen of Norway and Olga Alexeyeva of Russia, two of the sharper members of the consortium, now lay in straitjackets at the mental hospital in Salisbury, foaming at the mouth and speaking gibberish.

Madness is a known risk with this sort of investigation, Penny reminded herself. *They knew in advance the dangers they would face.*

She felt bad about it, but not that bad.

After all, I'm fine—just fine.

Some six months ago, though, a major breakthrough had been achieved, and Penny could hardly contain herself. Once they completed their mission in the months ahead, she knew the remaining investigators would be wealthy beyond their wildest dreams.

As she smugly sat in her tea shop, she knew her time of prosperity had come.

After laboring all these years, I deserve it.

Each day at this time, Penny thought through the cornucopia of options of what to do with her fifty million British pounds. Once she sold her modest home in Salisbury, she could go anywhere, she reckoned. *And at forty-five years of age, I have the world at my fingertips. Maybe I'll fly to Rio, buy a condominium and find a young Brazilian stud muffin to hang around with.*

But at five feet, two inches tall, weighing one hundred eighty pounds, and with stringy, thinning, shoulder-length brown hair, Penny knew she was no beauty by any stretch of the imagination.

But appearances don't mean anything as far as wealth is concerned. I'm certain I can find someone who would enjoy being around a woman of means, someone who would do anything to make me happy. She breathed in deeply as she thought about it. *Or maybe I'll fly to New York City and enjoy the finer things in life. Perhaps spend a few months at the Canyon Ranch Resort in Tucson, Arizona? Paris? Rome? The Seychelles?* She exhaled slowly. The possibilities were endless.

Penny squealed and jiggled with excitement. Her upcoming worldwide adventures seemed too good to be true. The task had taken twenty years, but it was worth it. She couldn't be happier.

After pulling down the shop window blinds, she stood and walked through partitioning curtains to a private room adjacent to the sales area. She couldn't wait any longer; she had to see, once again, her ticket to the good life.

Penny flipped over a portion of a large, multicolored Persian area rug, revealing a secret trap door. She pulled it open and carefully walked down creaky, wobbly wooden stairs to a dusty basement that reeked of mold. As she reached the bottom, she flipped on the light switch and stood before a red brick wall. She pushed a carefully concealed button, and the wall retracted, exposing a very large safe. Penny twirled the dials with the combination that only she knew, pulled on the handle, and with a *snap,* the safe popped open. Enormous wealth lay before her, and she was mesmerized.

Her silent worship of the stash was interrupted when she heard the front door rattle.

Don't they know I'm closed? she thought, irritated.

Then she heard the door crack open, and footsteps sounded on the level above her.

"What the bloody hell?" she said under her breath. Handguns were strictly controlled in the UK, but she kept an old Colt .45 revolver, smuggled in just for this sort of occasion. She had hoped never to use it.

But now, she was glad she had it in her hands. She pointed the muzzle of the gun at the stairwell and waited patiently.

The stairs creaked once again.

Penny clicked the hammer back, into its locked position.

"Stop," she warned with a snarl.

Then she noticed the strong odor of rotten eggs and vinegar, and a familiar face emerged from the shadowy stairs.

"Oh, it's you," she said in relief, and dropped the weapon to her side. "Why didn't you tell me you were coming? I would have been glad to have opened the d—"

The unexpected guest interrupted her with a raised, gloved hand that held a pistol—pointed directly at her.

"What are you doing?" she asked, shocked.

She began to lift her Colt again, but not before four shots pierced her head, chest and abdomen.

Penny Pumpernickel, popular proprietor of Teas of the World and keeper of international secrets, crumpled to the floor and died moments later, her eyes frozen open in disbelief.

Chapter 1

Daniel Fishinghawk sat at a handsome brown and black laminate desk in his comfortable new office in Hanga Roa, Easter Island, enjoying a quiet moment at his computer, when he heard a piercing scream from outside.

Daniel jumped to his feet.

A young Rapanui boy, who appeared to be around ten, wearing denim shorts and a white T-shirt with a picture of Boyz II Men on the front, flew through the door into his office.

"Are you Mister Hawk?" The boy was frantic and breathless.

Daniel knelt down to face him. "Yes, that is my name, and what is yours?"

"Apera Pakarati."

"What's going on, Apera Pakarati?"

"I need to hire you. Is this enough?" He slapped a one hundred Chilean peso note down on the table.

Daniel knew it was the equivalent of around seventeen U.S. cents, but he touched the note with reverence. "Consider me hired. Now, what do you need?"

"I want your help. Haumaka is gone!" Apera gripped Daniel's desk with both hands.

"Haumaka?"

"Yes, I can't find him anywhere. Come now!" He grabbed Daniel's hand and they rushed outside through the still-open door.

Daniel took a moment to slam it shut, then they ran along in silence. After sprinting for over ten minutes, they arrived at a small, corrugated metal-and-plywood home, painted a bright yellow, located on the outskirts of town.

Daniel paused at the entrance and caught his breath. "Don't you think we should let your parents know I'm with you before we go inside?"

"Father is not at home; he's at work. Mother has gone to the market. We must find Haumaka before she comes back. If we don't, I will be in big trouble."

Daniel asked, "What is Haumaka?"

"He's my pet snake?" Apera searched around the doorway as he spoke.

"Snake? What kind?" Daniel began to look around as well.

"Boa! Boa! Haumaka is my boa!"

"Boa constrictor? Isn't it against the law to have them on the island?" Daniel relaxed and placed a calming hand on Apera's shoulder.

"Yes, that is why I must find him soon—or my parents will make me get rid of him. I secretly bought him last year when we visited relatives in Santiago. He was only a baby snake then, and I sneaked him onto the island in my suitcase without my parents knowing about it."

Apera gulped, distraught. "It wouldn't take much for my father to take a hoe to him. Mr. Hawk, Haumaka and I love each other. We must find him."

Daniel chuckled. "Okay, let's go inside."

Apera led him through a partially open front door into the modest home with green linoleum floors and matching painted walls, to a small bedroom with bunk beds jammed into one corner. A large, glass aquarium, turned on its side, sat on the floor in the facing corner.

"You have a brother?" Daniel asked, as he briefly studied the bunk beds.

"Yes, how did you know?" Apera seemed astonished.

"Wild guess," Daniel said. "How old is he?"

"Eight. His name is Hehu."

"Where is he?"

"With my mother."

Daniel scanned the room. Using his photographic memory, which some call an eidetic memory, he took a picture of the scene in his mind, knowing he would remember it forever, in the minutest detail. He scrutinized the aquarium, a thirty-gallon size, with a wire screen lid with clamps. The lid was ajar, and the clamps were unscrewed.

Daniel took a deep breath through his nose. His grandfather had always said his sense of smell was akin to that of a bloodhound. This was one of the main reasons he was able to track the prolific serial killer of Easter Island.

A faint scent was noticeable, one Daniel was sure he could follow, even if he had worn a blindfold. Daniel thought for a moment and asked, "Is Haumaka a boy or a girl?"

Apera shyly confessed, "He's actually a girl."

Daniel already knew. When female boas are ready to mate, they have a distinctive odor, one that could be detected by male boas. Most humans would not have been able to appreciate the scent, but Daniel could.

"How long has he . . . she . . . been missing?"

"About thirty minutes."

"Good."

Daniel went to his hands and knees, keeping his nose inches from the floor. He followed the serpentine trail through the home and out of the front door. Once outside, he had slightly bent blades of grass to help him find the way, and he lifted his nose from the ground.

Apera crawled alongside him, sniffing wildly and copying Daniel's every move.

Daniel asked, "Did you leave the lid of the aquarium open?"

"No, I always close it tight."

"Does your brother like Haumaka?"

"No, he hates him . . . her. One day I put Hehu's pet rat in the cage with Haumaka so they could play. Before I could stop him . . . her, Haumaka gulped it down. My brother has never forgiven Haumaka—or me."

"I see. What do you usually feed her?"

Apera uncomfortably coughed before answering, "Rats."

Plenty of those around here, Daniel thought with a grin, thinking back to the time he ate them in old Rapa Nui.

Daniel's orderly mind quickly pieced things together . . . not that this was that hard to figure out: Apera gets mad at Hehu for some unknown reason; he intentionally puts his brother's pet rat in the aquarium to die a miserable death, much to his brother's displeasure; Hehu retaliates by opening the lid to the aquarium and tipping it over before he leaves with his mother, allowing Haumaka to escape.

Just like brothers.

After about a hundred feet of winding through the grassy terrain, they approached a neighbor's home, painted a bright purple.

Without warning, a loud shriek startled them.

Daniel and Apera jumped to their feet and ran toward the sound, which came from the back of the purple house. They discovered a middle-aged Rapanui woman who stood, paralyzed in fear, with what looked to be a ten-foot-long emerald green snake coiled around her right leg and abdomen, moving up to her chest, its tongue flicking in and out.

"Haumaka!" Apera shouted with delight as he ran up to the now screaming woman and uncoiled the snake from her. He kissed his reptile friend on its head.

"I'm sorry," he said to the woman, as he gleefully skipped away. "It won't happen again."

The woman said nothing. She was trembling from head to toe, unblinking eyes bulging as she stared straight ahead.

I suspect the bribery amount will be substantial, Daniel thought with a wry smile. *Apera will likely be taking out the garbage and scrubbing her floors for awhile.*

As Daniel and Apera walked back toward Apera's home, the boy said, "You are one great detective. You are worth every peso I paid you!"

Daniel laughed and patted Apera on the back.

After leaving Apera at his home, Daniel slowly strolled back to his office, enjoying the peaceful walk. When he reached the front door, he stopped to admire the wooden sign hanging beside it:

Daniel "Hawk" Fishinghawk, Jr.
Private Investigator
of the
Strange and Mysterious

Somehow, this case wasn't exactly what he had in mind when he had the sign carved, but what would tomorrow bring?

He looked at his watch. Mahina, his lovely wife, would be by soon.

Daniel sighed contentedly with the thought.

Chapter 2

From the front of his office, Daniel heard the phone ringing. He walked in, sat at his desk and picked it up.

"This is Hawk," Daniel said.

"Hawk, you ol' son-of-a-sea-cook, when are you going to give up that frickin' island and come back to work for the NYPD?"

"Kip Kelly!" Daniel exclaimed. "You never give up, do you?" Daniel leaned comfortably back in his chair.

"Give up? Are you freakin' kidding me? I'll never quit trying to get my favorite detective to come back to the place he loves more than anywhere. I figured by now you were getting tired of eating papayas, pineapple and mangos, and seeing all those half-naked dancers doing the hula. Besides, I'd bet my bottom dollar you've got diarrhea from all that tropical fruit, your sunburn is killing you and you have a food allergy from eating too much fish."

"Chief, I think you've got Easter Island mixed up with Hawaii." Daniel shook his head.

"The fargin' hell I do!" Kip Kelly shouted. "I know more about Polygonia than you think."

"Chief, it's Polynesia."

"That's what I frickin' meant!" Chief Kelly screamed into the phone.

Daniel could almost see his squinting, watery blue eyes, the veins bulging out on his forehead and his thinning grey hair. Daniel was certain the smell of cheap cigars still clung to his clothes. But there was something else . . . something new . . .

Daniel chuckled. "Chief, if you don't mind me saying so, I've noticed you're not using the *f* word like you used to."

"Damn, I was hoping you wouldn't notice. You see, after I gave a press conference couple of months ago, someone complained to Commissioner Walsh about my language. He pulled me aside and let me know, in no uncertain terms, that I had to change my way of putting things . . . or else."

"Or else . . . what?"

Kelly cleared his throat. "Let's just say that my next job would be something like dressing hot dogs at Coney Island."

After a moment of uncomfortable silence, Kelly added, "Okay, Hawk, here's my final offer. Commissioner Walsh has agreed to pay you *five* times what you used to make and give you two months paid vacation. You heard me right, *two months*. Hells bells, Hawk, you'll make more than the President of the United States. With all the money you'll have, I'll probably come to you for a loan some day!"

Daniel shook his head.

"Oh, by the way, Hawk, the grapevine tells me you got married. I've got to tell you that the women at the station are devastated. The Kimberly-Clark stock on the New York Stock Exchange has exploded upward, just from all the Kleenex they've sold. So, what's your new wife's name?"

"Mahina."

"What does that mean?"

"It's Rapanui for moon."

"Think about it, Hawk. And with all that time off, you can spend some of your hard-earned bucks lounging in the Caribbean with Moon Lady, sipping piña coladas and making eyes at each other."

Daniel chuckled again. *Some things never change.*

"Come on, Hawk, we're desperate. Do it for the sake of your fellow New Yorkers. Whaddya say?"

"Chief, I'm perfectly happy here. Thanks all the same."

Kip Kelly muttered, "Somehow, I knew that would be your answer. Since you've said no, I've got something else on the table that might interest you."

"What's that?"

"I just got a call this morning from Scotland Yard, in London, you know, from an Inspector Gordon Green, asking for you."

"Why me?"

"It seems the word has gotten around about your exploits on Easter Island, and they're wanting your help on some, well, unusual murders."

"What do you mean by unusual?" Daniel straightened in his chair.

"Ever heard of Stonehenge?"

Daniel's jaw dropped. "Why, yes, I've always wanted to see it."

"I'm told the first murder was there, and the rest have happened in a nearby town called Salisbury. I guess there's something strange going on; God knows what. The Brits are baffled, and that's saying something since they have some of the best bloody—as they say in England—detectives in the world. That is, except for the NYPD. But, hell, you already knew that. Green wouldn't give me the details, but I gave him your number and believe he'll be contacting you soon."

"Thanks for letting me know." Daniel was already searching his overfilled bookcase for a particular volume about famously mysterious places.

"Remember, if you change your mind—"

"You'll be the first to know," Daniel promised.

"I sure fargin' hope so," Kip Kelly responded, just before the phone went dead.

A short time later, Daniel heard a light tapping on the door.

"Come in," he called out.

Daniel's face lit up as he saw the most beautiful woman in the world, his wife Mahina, excitedly pop through the door. She was tall for a woman at around five feet eight inches, was in her early twenties, and had soft, dark hair that hung to just below her shoulders. Her Polynesian skin had an attractive, light-brown hue, and she had a shapely slender but strong build, with her shoulder width closely matching that of her hips. She wore a full-length, teal cotton dress and an ear-to-ear smile. She was gorgeous.

Mahina embraced her handsome husband, five years older than she and a bit taller. As always, because of his regular practice of yoga, strength training and aerobic exercise, he appeared toned and fit, and had neatly trimmed, short black hair.

"Dan-iel, I'm so happy to see you this evening," she murmured in Rapanui, as she lovingly studied him.

As Daniel looked at her, he still couldn't believe his good fortune. Who would have ever guessed that the love of his life would have come from Rapa Nui's distant past? And who could ever have predicted how well she would adapt to the modern world? As he heard her call his name, he was reminded how those in ancient Rapa Nui had difficulty pronouncing his name without a pause in the middle, and it warmed his heart to hear Mahina still speak his name that way.

"Mahina, I'm always glad to see you," he replied. His dark-brown eyes were fixed on her.

As she pulled up a chair in front of his desk, Daniel was certain he could not be happier. Mahina was as kind and as loving as anyone he had ever met.

Daniel also realized that both of them had been raised to think for themselves, to be strong and independent in their thoughts and actions. So, when both believed they were right, it occasionally led to a good-natured squabble. But they were good compromisers and almost always able to find a middle ground.

But that's the way life is, Daniel thought. *To believe things would be perfect was unrealistic. Perfection didn't exist in the real world. Ups and downs were to be expected—in anything and everything.*

After Mahina had settled into her chair, Daniel said, "Tell me about your day."

"It was wonderful. The children here are so bright and interested in the history of Rapa Nui. One child asked me, 'How do you know so much about long ago?' 'Oh,' I said, quite truthfully, 'I am from the past. I was the daughter of the *'ariki mau*, the ancient spiritual leader of Rapa Nui.'

"The children nearly fell out of their chairs laughing, but the other teacher in the room, who knew of my origins, had a smug look on her face and didn't breathe a word."

Daniel and Mahina both laughed at the thought.

She asked, "Tell me how things are with you."

"Very well. This morning I investigated a home that an elderly woman claimed was haunted with a spirit of the dead, an *akuaku*."

"Really?"

"Yes. It turns out that moaning sound she heard during the middle of the night was actually some neighborhood boys who were trying to scare her to death, and they almost succeeded. I found their footprints outside her bedroom window and was able to track them back to their homes. When I explained the situation to their parents, they were none too happy, and I believe the moaning will now stop."

Mahina winked and said, "Good job, Detective."

"And this afternoon, I rescued a woman from the clutches of a runaway boa constrictor."

"Sounds like you've had a most interesting day."

"I have." Daniel gestured to the phone. "And just a few moments ago, I received a call from my old detective boss in New York City, Chief Kip Kelly, telling me about some murders that have taken place around a spiritual place called Stonehenge, and wondering if I would help to solve them."

"What is Stonehenge?"

"It's a prehistoric monument in a land called England. It's where the English language comes from."

"Where is Eng-land?"

"It's a place far across the waters to the north, an island that is part of a group of countries called Europe."

"I see."

"Anyway, I've studied a little about Stonehenge, and it is England's greatest ancient temple. Would you like to see a picture of it?"

"I'd love to." Mahina rose to get a good look.

Daniel pulled up an image on his computer and showed it to her as she walked behind him. She put her hands on his back as she looked over his shoulder.

"Oh Dan-iel," she said, eyes wide. "It is stunning."

"Isn't it, though? I'd love to see it, even if I have to perform an investigation to do so. I have yet to hear the details, but if it all works out, are you interested in going with me?"

"You mean get into an airplane and fly over the ocean?" Mahina faked a frown.

"Yes."

She kissed him on the forehead and spoke softly, "I'd love to see the world with you—especially that place. There's something magical and mysterious about it. I am not sure about you, but it calls to me."

"I couldn't agree more. With that settled, what would you like to have for dinner?"

The phone rang, and Daniel answered.

"Hello. Okay. I understand. We'll meet you there."

"Who was that?" Mahina asked.

Daniel's voice sounded slightly strained. "That was Tiare. She said she needs to speak with us. It sounded serious. She asked if we could meet at Laguna Azul for dinner. Is that all right with you?"

"You know how much I love Laguna Azul. Let's go."

Daniel stood and together they went out the front door, and Daniel turned to lock the door behind them. They strolled into the warm evening air, walking hand in hand, and Daniel couldn't help but wonder what Tiare had on her mind. After hearing the gravity in her voice, Daniel was certain it was something important—very important.

I love my life, here on Rapa Nui. Will what Tiare has to say somehow change things? His sixth sense rose up to haunt him.

He somehow knew, no, he was certain . . . what he was about to hear would present challenges, ones he wasn't sure he was prepared to face.

Chapter 3

When Daniel and Mahina arrived at the Laguna Azul restaurant, they found their dear friend Tiare waiting expectantly at an outside table covered with a yellow tablecloth. Tiare looked as chipper, healthy and alert as she always did, belying her ninety-five years. Her face was wrinkled, yet she appeared far younger than her actual age. Her white hair was neat and closely trimmed, and she wore matching navy-blue shirt and pants. A seashell wind chime jingled melodically in the background.

Daniel had sensed anxiety in Tiare's voice when he spoke with her on the phone, and now he noted a look of worry on her face that could not be cloaked by her radiant appearance.

Tiare gestured to chairs at the table. She spoke in Rapanui, the language they all knew. "Daniel, Mahina, please join me."

"We'd love to," they answered in unison. They took turns hugging her before they sat.

"You'll be pleased to hear that the menu offers a new special tonight." Tiare handed them menus. "Barbecued tempeh sandwiches on whole wheat buns, along with a side salad. I'm certainly going to have it."

Mahina asked, "What is tempeh?"

"Tempeh is a fermented soy product," Tiare explained, "and is an excellent protein and dietary fiber source. Mahina, since you're considering becoming a vegetarian, it is a food you should try."

"I'd love to. Dan-iel?"

"Make it three," he said.

Tiare said, "Daniel, you have always treated me when we come here, but this is a special occasion, and I want to pay."

"Fair enough," Daniel conceded, "but only if I get to buy next time."

"Sounds fair," Tiare agreed.

Their order was placed, and they were sipping iced hibiscus tea when Tiare announced, "I have some news to share with both of you. An important decision must soon be made."

"Tell us," Mahina said, wrinkles forming across her brow.

Tiare began, "Loved ones, as the last living shaman of the Rapanui, it is well past time for me to choose a successor. Mahina, as I'm sure you know, the Rapanui have, and always will, need a shaman to guide them."

"Certainly," Mahina confirmed.

"Over the past ten years, this issue has been a pressing concern for me, but in spite of looking diligently and repeatedly at all of my kinsman, as well as children born to them, there was not one who, according to my estimation, met the stringent requirements to be a shaman."

"And what are those?" Daniel asked.

"The pathway of the shaman is most difficult, and the candidate for being a shaman must be very strong to face the challenges with which they will invariably be confronted.

"As you know, Daniel, my main functions as a shaman have been of the ways of healing, and especially dreaming, entering the world of spirit. But there are many other potential pathways for the shaman. These include being a storyteller, a keeper of folk memory, a spiritual advisor and a dream interpreter. In addition, anyone who wishes to be a shaman must be able to walk effortlessly between the physical and the spiritual worlds, and those who are unable to find that balance risk insanity.

"Besides all this," Tiare continued, "the main focus of a shaman's life has to be centered on their people. Their own personal needs and the needs of their families cannot be placed above their sacred duties as a shaman."

Feeling uneasy, Daniel asked, "Why are you telling us all this?"

Tiare closed her eyes for a second and sighed. "Because, Daniel, not too long ago I sat in deep meditation and asked for guidance from my animal spirit guide, Honu. She made it quite clear to me who was the best candidate to be the next shaman of the Rapanui."

"And?" Mahina folded her hands on the table top.

Tiare warmly put her hand on Mahina's shoulder and answered, "You, sister—you."

"What?" Daniel blurted out.

Mahina looked bewildered.

At that moment the food was served on turquoise-colored plates, and they ate in silence.

Daniel was astonished and could barely eat his meal, in spite of how delicious it tasted. He reached under the table and squeezed Mahina's hand.

She squeezed his in return.

He scooted his chair next to hers and put his arm around her.

Tiare drew in a deep breath and said, "I have more to share. Are you ready to hear?"

Daniel and Mahina glanced at each other and nodded.

"I know my words are hard for you to hear, but there is more you must know. I was led by Honu to believe that there was danger in this undertaking, not only for me, but also for Mahina, if you chose to be my apprentice. It is my belief that this danger is so great that both of our lives could be at risk—"

"Impossible," Daniel angrily interrupted, shaking his head back and forth. "I've looked too hard and long for Mahina. She's too important to me to take the chance of losing her. Can't we just say no and wait until some other candidates make themselves known?"

"Of course you can decide not to choose this pathway," Tiare said in a calming voice, "and I would understand if you did so. The risk is that I might die before a suitable person appears, and forever the Rapanui would be without a shaman."

Tiare looked at Mahina and quietly asked, "What are your thoughts on this?"

"I must have time to think."

"I understand," Tiare said. "I must say more. Mahina, if you decide to take this journey with me, I will require your full attention. How long this will take, I do not know; it all depends upon how quickly you progress. And so, Daniel, I know you have only been married for ten months, yet you must step to the side for a period of time."

"But I must stay with her to help protect from the danger," Daniel protested.

"I understand your concern. But you should know that, together, Mahina and I are strong, and I am confident that whatever danger awaits us, we can withstand it. I believe that those who undergo the shamanic journey are always protected to some degree, but there are no guarantees. The reason I have discussed this with both of you is because this must be a joint decision, and if indeed you choose to move forward, I'm afraid you both will have to sacrifice an enormous amount. It is my fondest hope that the decision will be made for Mahina to take the pathway to shamanism, but please know that whatever you choose will not diminish my love for you. Do you have any questions?"

Mahina answered first. "Not at this time. Dan-iel and I will ponder what you've said, and we should be able to let you know of our decision within the next few days."

Daniel was clearly rattled but concurred, saying, "That should give us enough time."

Tears came into Tiare's eyes as she saw the stunned looks on their faces. She knew she had given them an impossible decision to make.

One that had no right answer.

Chapter 4

The next morning, Daniel sat thinking at the desk in his office, blankly staring at the packed bamboo bookcase standing against the opposite wall. Many of his favorite titles were jammed into it, including Tolkien's *The Lord of the Rings*, Paramahansa Yogananda's *Autobiography of a Yogi*, *Kitchen Table Wisdom* by Rachel Naomi Remen, and many others. He loved reading, and as a speed reader, he devoured at least five books a week, sometimes more. Daniel preferred the organic feel and smell of a book, as opposed to e-books, and voraciously read as many as he could get his hands on, which was no easy task on Rapa Nui.

But for now, books were the last thing on his mind. Last night, he and Mahina drove home in silence. They both had a restless night, and when they woke, neither was ready to talk about the decision that needed to be made. After they kissed goodbye, Daniel headed to his office, and she to the elementary school to teach.

Daniel had much to ponder. He knew Mahina was a capable woman who had an unprecedented knowledge of ancient times, yet the idea of his love being confronted with danger, when he would not be around to help, was almost too much to bear. He understood the duty she felt to her people, the Rapanui, but being a teacher was one thing, and if she became a shaman, Tiare had been clear that her responsibility to her people would increase.

How much am I willing to share her with others?

The phone rang.

"Hello."

"Hello," a heavily accented British voice replied, "My name is Chief Detective Gordon Green, Scotland Yard, and I'm calling from London. Is this Daniel . . . Fishinghawk?"

"It is."

"Two years ago, I met your former superior, Chief Detective Kip Kelly of the New York Police Department, at an international conference in Paris on contemporary murder and assassination. Sponsored by Interpol, one of the results of our meeting resulted in Internet sharing of information between countries to solve crimes. Chief Detective Kelly said I should call you . . . Hawk."

"Yes, please."

"Hawk, may I trust that Chief Detective Kelly told you I'd be giving you a ring?"

"He did."

"Excellent. As you know, I'm calling about some murders that are taking place here, in England. What have you been told?"

"Very little."

"Understood. I will give you a brief sketch. There have been four murders so far. The first was an unarmed guard at Stonehenge who was killed just over a year ago. Usually three guards are on duty, but two had the night off, and I suspect our killer somehow knew that. The poor chap was shot through the heart and died instantly. His body was found stretched out on top of the Slaughter Stone—"

"What?" Daniel interrupted.

"The Slaughter Stone, which sits at the entrance to Stonehenge. It originally was upright but now lies flat. It has shallow surface depressions that collect rainwater, and the water reacts with iron in the stone, giving a rusty—some in the past thought it bloody—appearance. Some barmy—"

"Barmy?"

"Crazy. Some barmy chap in the late seventeenth century thought it was evidence of human sacrifice in ancient times, so he named it the Slaughter Stone, but he was off his trolley—"

"Off his trolley?"

Green answered with a chuckle, "Again, crazy. Actually, our guard was shot and killed in the *center* of Stonehenge but was later dragged onto the stone. Our murderer has a beastly sense of humor, that's for sure."

"Sounds like it."

"Another interesting thing," Green continued. "One of the bluestones—a type of stone at Stonehenge—was stolen at the same time. That seems to be the reason for that killing, but we ask, 'Why would someone perform murder to get one, especially since they could obtain a similar stone from the Preseli Hills in Wales—the original source of the Stonehenge bluestones—without murdering a soul?'"

"Odd," commented Daniel. "What about the other murders?"

"The other three people were shot and killed in the nearby town of Salisbury, beginning some four months ago. The first was a tea shop owner, followed by two others."

"What makes you think that the murder at Stonehenge is connected to the killings in Salisbury?"

"The ballistics match on the bullets in all of the victims. The murder weapon is a Glock pistol, Austrian made. Once we find the weapon, we find the killer."

"Anything else?" asked Daniel.

"Well, there is another quite odd thing—extremely odd, really. Each of the last three killed had quite large safes tucked away in hidden locations in their homes."

"Really?"

"Yes, and not only were they emptied of their contents, but also the inside surfaces of each of the safes were meticulously wiped clean by our murderer, so forensics has no clue whatsoever what they stored."

"Curious," Daniel said. "Do you have any idea why?"

"None at all. For some reason, the killer did not want us to know what was kept there." He paused for a moment. "We have learned from Interpol records that you have a knack for figuring out . . . unusual . . . cases such as this. Chief Detective Kelly posted online, in the program we share with Interpol, that you possess special expertise and skill in discovering that which is deemed undiscoverable. We need your help. Might you be interested in coming here to assist us?"

"Could be. I'll need to give it some thought."

"Right," Green said. "In addition, just last week our government approved a reward of five million British pounds to anyone who can solve these murders. Everyone here is bloody well worked up over these killings, the locals are frightened, the tourists are avoiding the area, and if we don't get to the bottom of this soon, Salisbury will become—as you Americans might put it—a ghost town. Hawk, our people are neither accustomed to nor fascinated by gun violence, like Americans seem to be, if we are to believe the media. So, if you decide to pitch in and help us, I'll tell you more details once you arrive. Let me know when you make up your mind."

"I will."

"Jolly good. Bye."

Daniel hung up the phone. He had to admit, he was intrigued by these murders and wouldn't mind having a crack at solving them. He enjoyed figuring out the simple cases here on Rapa Nui, but he yearned for something more challenging, something he could dig his investigative teeth into.

But he couldn't imagine going to England without Mahina; if she chose the difficult path of the shaman, she would likely opt to stay in Rapa Nui. With Tiare's advanced age, Mahina's training should begin as soon as possible. It might be best for him not to be here; the shaman path was not a group affair.

The reward for finding the killer was also a factor, he had to admit, even if only to himself. *Mahina and I live simply and are financially comfortable,* but an additional five million British pounds, plus the twenty million American dollars already raised by the sale of the *rongorongo* board Mahina brought through time, would assist in completing the institute. This proposed establishment would help Rapa Nui deal with the many issues that confronted it, such as pollution, protecting the ancient *moai* and *ahus*, and accelerating the process of reforestation.

Daniel's face lit up as he thought about the institute. Last year, when he and Mahina returned from their visit to Oklahoma, a meeting of the Rapanui community was arranged. As he expected, the project was enthusiastically received and the community voted to name it the Hotu Matu'a Institute, after the legendary founder of Rapa Nui. A committee was set up to oversee the design and eventual construction. Tiare was unanimously chosen to head the group, and included among the ten other members selected were Alame Koreta of the Te Manutara Hotel, Mahina and, surprisingly, Roberto Ika, the paranoid schizophrenic who was originally accused of the murders on Rapa Nui. Despite his mental disability, with Roberto's selection, Daniel realized how popular he was in the community.

The phone rang again.

"Hello."

"Mr. Hawk?"

"Yes?"

"This is Apera Pakarati. Haumaka has gotten out again. Can you help me find her?"

"I'll be there in a few minutes."

Before he walked out the door, he grinned, and a bit of weight was lifted from his shoulders.

I love my job.

Daniel and Mahina both arrived late at their cozy rental home, which, like Tiare's, was constructed of native volcanic rock. After a brief meal of leftover steamed vegetables on a bed of pasta and cheese, they went straight to bed. Six hours later, at three a.m., Daniel was still awake—too much was on his mind. He took a moment to look lovingly at Mahina as she lay beside him, bed covers pulled up to her neck. He brushed her long, dark hair from her face and saw her open her eyes. Apparently, she was having as much trouble falling asleep as he was.

"Mahina, my love, are you awake?"

"Yes," she said.

"What's on your mind?" Daniel asked.

"Dan-iel, you do know how much I love you, don't you?"

"I do, Mahina. And you know I love you too."

"I feel your love every day, Dan-iel. I have never doubted it—not once."

She sat up in bed, surrounded by the full moon's glow that lit the room through the open window. A cool breeze gently blew through her hair.

"Do you remember our wedding vows?"

"How could I ever forget?"

"I am thinking in particular of the words, 'I promise to support your spiritual path, wherever it leads you, however difficult it is.' My love, do you still hold to these vows?"

"I do."

"Then you should know that I must choose the path of the shaman. My people need me. But I also want you to be aware of my devotion to you and our future children, if we are so blessed, and I will do all I can to find a balance between my public and personal responsibilities. I also recall more words from our vows: 'I promise to love you, as long as my eyes see the sunshine, my feet feel the earth and my hair is blown by the wind.' I take these promises very seriously."

Daniel felt warmed by her words. "As do I."

"Now, Dan-iel, do you desire to go to Eng-land—to Stonehenge—to investigate the murders there?"

"I do, but I am concerned about leaving you and Tiare to face the danger by yourselves. I feel like I would be leaving you in your time of need."

"Dan-iel, do you doubt the strength that I have?"

"Not at all."

"Then I want you to go. You have your own life purpose to fulfill, and I don't want to get in the way of that. When would you be leaving?"

Daniel gulped. "Probably in the next week or so."

Mahina's face shined in the moonlight as she lay back down beside him. "Then we have a lot of lovemaking to do before you leave, wouldn't you say?"

Daniel pulled her close, feeling her soft, warm skin next to his. He inhaled deeply. He imprinted in his mind her fragrant scent, the scent he first appreciated on old Rapa Nui.

He murmured, "I couldn't agree more."

He kissed her soft, pliant lips and tenderly caressed her soft breasts, feeling his passion build. He became lost in the moment, knowing that all too soon his memories of these times would be all he would have to sustain him.

Mahina will be a world away.

Chapter 5

Daniel, in blue jeans and a loose fitting long-sleeved white shirt, sat next to Mahina, who wore a flowing, sea green dress. They were at the crowded Mataveri International Airport in Hanga Roa, waiting for Daniel to be called for his flight to Santiago, Chile. From there he would fly to London.

Sitting across from them was Tiare, dressed in black, along with Alame Koreta and her husband, Jack Daldy, of the Te Manutara Hotel. Alame, an attractive middle-aged woman with a youthful and assured presence, had mid-length, wavy brown hair and wore a short, rust-colored floral-dress. Her Kiwi husband, Jack, in his late sixties, had sandy hair and wore a matching khaki shirt and shorts.

Daniel's instincts were screaming at him. *Something about this seems wrong, very wrong.* Yet, he knew the die was cast, and barring an act of God, he would soon be on the plane, leaving his love and Tiare to fend for themselves.

Daniel thought back to the recent events. After he and Mahina had made their decisions a week ago for her to begin her shaman training and for him to travel to England, Daniel had contacted Inspector Green, who had made all of the travel arrangements. Daniel was to meet him first in London and then together they would travel to Salisbury, where he would stay until the case was solved.

Alame stood, as did Daniel, hugged him and said in Rapanui, "Daniel, please come back safe and sound. You are very important to the Rapanui."

Jack also stood and shook Daniel's hand. In English, he said, "Come back soon, mate."

Daniel nodded at them as they turned to leave.

After Daniel sat, Tiare leaned over and whispered to him, "Daniel, I know you are concerned about leaving us, but I want to assure you that we will be as safe as possible. Also know that I have dreamed about your upcoming adventure, and I feel certain that you will face at least as much danger as we will. The best advice I can give you is, when you are challenged, take moments in meditation, listen to your inner voice and answers will come to you—some of which will defy logic. But listen anyway."

"I will."

"Do you remember," Tiare asked, "when I said that in many ways you are like a shaman?"

"I do."

"As I told you then, you sense and understand things others cannot. I am sure you already realize that. So I advise that the next time you sit in contemplation, seek out your animal guide."

"Animal guide?"

"Yes, animal guide," Tiare said in low tones. "To this point, you've done quite well in your dreaming, but there likely will come a time when you might need some assistance, just like when your grandfather and parents came back into your life. Knowing your nickname, and your past history, I believe you already know what animal it is."

Of course I know, Daniel realized, thinking back to the spirit animal his parents chose to be when he was young.

The hawk.

Tiare seemed to read his thoughts and winked at him. "Good," she said, "Now—"

Suddenly a bare-chested, aged Rapanui man, with long and matted grey hair and a feral, crazy stare, staggered into the waiting area from the outside. A large gecko was perched on his right shoulder. The man jerked his head back and forth, scanning the room, and screamed out, "Fishinghawk! Where's Fishinghawk?"

A security guard quickly moved in and grabbed him by the arm. "Sir," he said. "Come with me."

The wild man jerked his arm away and yelled louder, "Fishinghawk! Fishinghawk!"

Daniel hurried to the guard and calmly said, "Don't worry, he's harmless. If you don't mind, I'll take care of this."

The guard looked relieved and walked away, shaking his head.

"Roberto Ika!" Daniel exclaimed, as he led him to where Mahina and Tiare stood. "What are you doing here?"

Roberto grabbed Daniel in a fierce hug, and then, in a gentler fashion, embraced Mahina and Tiare.

He announced, "I'd like all of you to meet my gecko friend, Spirit."

As if on cue, Spirit looked at them and chirped. Daniel couldn't help but grin.

"I was lying in bed last night," Roberto said, "and when I woke early this morning, I discovered he was lying asleep on my chest. We have already bonded, and he loves hanging around on my shoulder. He might be only a gecko, but he's very, very smart."

"Now, Daniel, I've heard that you're headed across the ocean to solve more murders. Is that right?

"It is."

"Before you leave, have you heard the big news?"

"No."

"Well," Roberto said quietly, as if being monitored, "I've got wind that the Inner Earth people are soon going to invade us."

"Who are the Inner Earth people?" Daniel struggled to keep a straight face.

Roberto looked exasperated. "Don't you know? They're the civilization that lives in the core of the Earth. They originally came from outer space and are jealous of us. They have green skin and weapons that would melt the flesh right off your bones."

"Really?"

Roberto glanced around the room and said, "Yes. They're planning to come out of caves and attack soon, and you know how many caves we have here on Rapa Nui. All the more places they can enter our world."

Daniel looked over at Mahina and Tiare. Mahina looked shocked, and Tiare seemed amused.

"Anyway, that's not the reason I came to see you off." He then leaned over and whispered softly, in an oddly sane and matter-of-fact tone of voice, "I just wanted you to know that I will never forget what you have done for me by getting me out of the house for crazy people in Santiago. While you're gone, I will keep an eye on things. Do not worry. You can count on me."

He slapped Daniel on the back and resumed his loud, lunatic voice, saying, "Those Inner Earth creatures I was telling you about? They better not try to come out here, because I am *ready* for them!"

"That's good to know," Daniel said, feeling confused.

Tiare pulled Daniel near. "I will miss you, my friend. Be careful and remember my words."

Stepping away from Daniel, she winked at him and Mahina then grabbed Roberto by the hand.

"Will you and Spirit come outside with me?" Tiare said, as she steered him to the entrance. "I would like to hear more about those invaders."

Roberto grinned like a character from *One Flew Over the Cuckoo's Nest*. "There is nothing I would like better. Bye, Daniel."

"Bye, Roberto."

Overhead, Daniel and Mahina heard a Spanish-accented announcement: *LAN Flight 461 to Santiago, now boarding*. Daniel felt his eyes well with tears and he pulled Mahina close to him. He could see tears forming in her eyes as well. He memorized the feel of her body.

"Mahina," he whispered, "soon you will undertake the path of the shaman. Know that my love will be with you on your journey."

"Dan-iel," she affectionately responded, "my love will be with you as well." She handed him a small white envelope. "Think of me when you hold this in your hands."

Final boarding—LAN Flight 461.

They tightly embraced and then parted. Daniel slowly walked away, glancing back frequently until Mahina was no longer in view.

Daniel entered the plane and found his seat. After placing his backpack under the seat in front of him, he looked out the window and saw Mahina, Tiare and Roberto standing together, waving, even though he knew they could not see him. He waved back as the plane pulled away.

When the plane was airborne, he opened the envelope Mahina had given him. In it was a pressed red hibiscus flower, one Daniel knew she had worn on their wedding day. Daniel prayed, with all his heart, that this would not be the last time he saw Mahina. He wished he could be sure, but he wasn't. Part of him wanted to turn the plane around and go back to Rapa Nui.

But he knew he couldn't.

In a dark, dreary cave on Rapa Nui, an evil presence gleefully rejoiced: *A major obstacle to my success is now gone.*

The time—*his* time—was approaching.

His sinister cackle echoed through the cave.

Chapter 6

Daniel sat restlessly on the plane, melancholy and trying to point his mind in the direction of his upcoming case.

But he couldn't, too much was on his mind.

His transfer in Santiago went without a hitch, and after a relatively short layover of two hours, he was off to London. He knew he needed to sleep but was unable to. His total flight time from Santiago to London was seventeen hours, and after a stopover in Madrid, his arrival in London was scheduled for 4:20 in the afternoon. The following day he would meet with Chief Inspector Green.

The plane was crowded, and he felt like a sardine squeezed into a tin. Daniel was in a window seat, but it didn't help that the man next to him had the physique of an overweight pro football lineman. One of his hairy, burly arms hung well over the armrest into Daniel's space.

For now, Daniel allowed his mind to flash randomly back to scenes etched in his consciousness. He saw himself walking alongside his Cherokee grandpa, Hunter Fishinghawk, tracking in the rolling Oklahoma hills east of Tahlequah. He relaxed as he once again relived the memory of his tall, strong grandpa, salt-and-pepper hair tied behind his head in a small ponytail. He'd taught Daniel the intricate secrets of Nature and the interconnectedness that she shared with humankind.

Daniel grimaced as his mind switched to a gruesome scene, one in which his grandpa's body had been ravaged by what he thought at the time were wild animals.

He later discovered that at least part of the damage had been caused by the evil shaman, Paoa, who had ventured from the past into the present in a futile attempt to kill Daniel.

Enough of that, he thought. He readjusted himself in his seat and slowed his breath.

Daniel redirected his mind to the first time he laid eyes upon Tiare, his dear friend who helped him in his quest to find the monstrous serial killer—later discovered to be Paoa, who had stalked, murdered and cannibalized tourists on Rapa Nui. Daniel warmly pictured Tiare's John Lennon glasses and her incessant desire to learn new things on the computer, even though at the time she was ninety-four years old.

Most folks her age are ready to be sedentary, thought Daniel, *but not Tiare. She was a living example of how to age gracefully.*

When they first met, she had already learned Spanish and English online, and, of course, she was already fluent in her native Rapanui tongue. Her fondness for Daniel fostered a desire to learn the Cherokee language, and she had found an online site to help her learn. Much to Daniel's great surprise, on occasion she would blurt out a simple phrase in Cherokee.

Revisiting his first meeting with Tiare had relaxed him. Daniel sighed.

I'll never forget the moment I first saw Mahina . . . He almost chuckled. *I was tied up, stripped and was lying naked on my back when she compassionately looked down at me. How blessed I am that she was willing to leave everything behind—to come from the past into the present—to be with me.*

Now, with Tiare's guiding hand, she was to begin on a path to become a shaman for the Rapanui people. In spite of her reassurances, Daniel could not put aside his concern about how this change might affect their relationship, not to mention Tiare's warning about a danger that faced them . . .

I refuse to be pulled into those thoughts. Daniel turned in his seat to stare out of the window, seeing nothing but billowing white clouds and a calm, deep blue sea.

His eyes misted with tears as he fondly thought of his friends from old Rapa Nui, Pakia and Uka, the gentle fishing folk who took him in and helped him survive in that primitive time. Daniel's mind strayed to Ropata, his comrade, who died at the hands of the skeleton-tattooed Atamu, the warrior Daniel initially mistook to be the tourists' murderer.

His mind moved to the ethereal visitation he'd experienced from his parents, who, along with his grandpa, had patiently watched over him through the years, refusing to go into the afterlife until they were assured that he was past the mortal danger Paoa posed.

I only hope that their current existence, whatever that might be, is peaceful. Certainly they deserve it after all those years of service to me. His right hand moved to his neck—a long-standing habit.

Daniel fingered the small brown-leather bag hanging there. It contained the bone fishhook given to him by Pakia and Uka, the two caracara feathers left behind by his parents, and his grandpa's green arrowhead, the one with an image of a hawk on it. Touching these objects filled Daniel with a sense of love and connectedness.

He hung on the verge of sleep, but his usually ordered and analytical mind was scattered and in disarray. Too many thoughts—too many concerns—crowded his consciousness. After what seemed like an eternity of trying not to hear crying babies, snoring and idle chatter, he fell into a troubled sleep and quickly began to dream.

    He was hiking on a rocky path, the Mid-Alamo Trail, one of his favorites, that crossed the rugged but beautiful canyons and mesas of Bandelier National Monument in northern New Mexico, an area that was one of the homes of the Ancestral Pueblos. Every time he visited, he felt reconnected to his Native American roots.

    Many ancient dwellings remained intact, built from niches that had been carved in the volcanic tuff. As he hiked, he saw scattered throughout the park, brightly painted pottery shards, hundreds of years old and oozing with the energy of their creators. He admired but did not disturb them.

    Daniel had already crossed both the Frijoles and Lummis Canyons, and as he topped a rise, looming before him was the mammoth, awe-inspiring Alamo Canyon. He inhaled deeply as he saw it. The gaping chasm still amazed him, no matter how many times he had seen it.

    Daniel descended into the canyon. He had taken this trail numerous times in the past and took each step carefully. One misstep and he would fall over the precipice to certain death.

After some twenty minutes, he climbed down the six hundred-foot descent to the canyon's floor and began the strenuous ascent up the other side. After much exertion and copious sweat, he emerged from the back side of Alamo Canyon. He started on his way to explore the nearby Yapashi Ruins and the magnificent carved Stone Lions.

All at once, a beautiful bird with gorgeous plumage, much like that of a peacock, landed in front of him. Daniel was amazed. The bird was very large and displayed a striking tail of gold and scarlet. It gathered a large nest of twigs around it, which unexpectedly ignited, and the bird screeched in agony as it was burned to ashes.

Smoke and the odor of burning flesh filled the air, and before long, Daniel saw something move in the smoldering embers. He carefully studied it, and he was shocked when a baby bird, a much smaller version of the large bird, emerged from the ashes and squawked loudly.

The phoenix, he thought with amazement, remembering his previous reads of Greek mythology.

To his surprise, he heard Mahina's voice calling to him from across the great expanse of the canyon.

"Dan-iel, my love!" she yelled, her voice echoing across to him. "I've been looking for you. I need your help. I'm in danger!"

"Mahina!" he screamed as loudly as he could, hoping she would be able to hear him.

To his dismay, Daniel saw an amorphous and undulating pitch-black blob moving close to her from behind. Even from this distance, he could hear an odd mixture of gurgling, sloshing and buzzing sounds.

"Look out!" he yelled.

Mahina turned around and shrieked as she saw the creature approach her. She tried to run away, but the mass oozed onto and around her. In moments, it had engulfed her entire body, and only her head protruded.

"Dan-iel!" she screamed, in agony. "Dan-iel! Help me! Please help me!"

Daniel stared, his heart in his throat, not knowing what to do. "Hang on, my love. I'm coming!"

As he climbed frantically back down the wall, there was a sudden, dead silence. He looked for Mahina, but she was gone, and only the dark form remained.

Wicked laughter echoed into the canyon from the vile creature, one that could have come from the depths of Hell.

Daniel screamed at the top of his lungs, "Nooooooooo!"

He screamed again, over and over, until he had no voice...

Daniel felt muscled arms shaking him.

"Hey, buddy, you okay?"

Daniel looked up to see his large seat mate staring at him with concern. All of the other passengers around him had turned in their seats to look.

"I'm fine," Daniel said as he straightened in his chair. "Just a bad dream, that's all."

As the others went back to their books, laptops and onboard movies, Daniel sat in stunned silence. Naturally, he was curious about what the image of the phoenix meant, but in his mind was one powerful, overriding concern.

Mahina.

Oh, God, Mahina...

What have I done?

Chapter 7

In the early morning, Mahina and Tiare sat cross-legged at each other's side in the sand of the east-facing Ovahe Beach. Mahina had only recently received her driver's license, and earlier she had driven Tiare to this beach in her and Daniel's used blue Toyota RAV-4.

The sun was just peeping over the horizon as they looked across the calm ocean. Ovahe was about one and a half kilometers southeast of 'Anakena, and with its turquoise water, pink sand and red scoria cliffs, was one of the most lovely beaches in the world. Yet, given its remote location, it was also one of the most inaccessible.

Mahina couldn't count the times she had been here in ancient Rapa Nui. Her clan, the Miru, loved coming here and swimming in the pristine waters, yet they rarely did, as the location was too close to their enemies, the eastern clans. Only with warriors at hand did they dare venture here.

She remembered how her little brothers, Kai and Poki, would squeal with delight as they splashed and dived in the sparkling, clear waters.

"Mahina, are you ready to begin your journey of being a shaman?" Tiare asked without taking her eyes off the horizon.

"Yes, teacher."

"Then one of the first skills you must learn is that of meditation. Only after you learn how to attain deep relaxation will you be able to travel in your nonmaterial body and develop your spiritual sight. Do you understand?"

"I do."

As a soft, warm wind blew in their faces, Tiare turned and said, "My inner voice tells me you have meditated before. Who was your teacher?"

"My father, Hotu Iti, the *'ariki mau*. He taught me the sacred practice."

"Ah, yes," Tiare said. "I should have known. Now, the most common method is that of listening to your breath. Is that what you learned?"

"It was."

"Then, much of what I tell you will be repetitive, so forgive me for telling you things you may already know. First, I must share with you that the practice is more than simply listening to your breath, it's putting your *full* concentration on it. Invariably, there will be distractions that might call your attention away from your breath: You could hear the call of seabirds and wish to listen to them; insects may buzz in your face or crawl on you. Instinct would have you brush them away, but as you meditate, such actions should be placed aside. Individuals might enter your quiet space while talking to each other, and children may scream and cry. When these disturbances attempt to intrude, smile at the distractions and allow them to push you deeper into meditation."

Tiare paused. "Do you understand so far?"

Mahina nodded without looking at her. "I do."

"Everyone's experience in meditation is different," Tiare explained. "What you need to face most will make itself known to you. Often, the first sessions will confront you with your greatest areas of discomfort. Of necessity, you must clear these before you can move forward in your training. Whatever you see, whatever you discover, remember that I, as your teacher, will be with you. Soon, very soon, there will come a time when you shall journey out on your own, but not now. Shall we begin?"

"I'm ready."

"Close your eyes, keep your mouth closed, and feel your breath move into your nose, the back of your throat and finally into your lungs, then back out the way it came."

Tiare turned to watch Mahina for a few moments before also closing her eyes. "Let us do this for awhile, and then I will instruct you further."

After some time, Tiare spoke. "Mahina, as you breathe, focus on that tiny instant between the in and the out breath. Don't hold your breath there; just make special note of that place."

Mahina did as she was told, and before long the waking world was gone to her. She no longer heard the crashing of waves, calls of the sea birds, or felt the sun on her face. All that was present was her breath, flowing in and out . . . and an enveloping peace.

Suddenly, she was rocked by the sounds of warfare, and she discovered she was observing a pitched battle at 'Anakena.

Mahina wondered: *Mother, father, Kai, Poki . . . are you all right?*

As she ran across the rocky ground toward her old home, the thrown spears and rocks passed right through her, and broken, men, women and children—some alive, some dead—lay all around. A loud *thud* sounded, and she discovered the Ahu Ature Huki, the ancient moai at Anakena, had been pulled over. Mahina was saddened by this horrific act, but was more concerned about her family.

She increased her pace.

A faint whisper from a somehow-familiar voice sounded in her head: *Mahina, listen to me. What you are seeing is not real; it is an illusion.*

Mahina shook her head and thought: *Of course it's real.*

Mahina dashed over to her old home and saw her father, Hotu Iti, the *'ariki mau*, sprawled out in front, impaled with three spears in his chest and one in his abdomen, his head cradled in the lap of his beautiful wife, Tavake. He looked older than when she had left with Dan-iel. His white feather headdress was knocked to the ground beside him, and the carved wooden ornaments that hung from his neck were covered with blood. He was pale, too pale, and he was breathing shallowly.

Mahina leaned over him, and as she did, the odor of fresh blood wafted into her face.

"Father, can you hear me?"

No response.

"Mother, can you?"

Tavake grimaced at her husband without any recognition of Mahina's presence. Hotu Iti weakly brushed Tavake's hair from her face, which was streaked with tears.

He whispered, "My dear, I am soon leaving this world. What of Kai and Poki?"

Tavake wailed, "They are both dead. They wait for you to join them in the land of spirit."

Hotu Iti grunted, then managed to say, "And join them I will." He mumbled, "Mahina—if only I could say goodbye to her."

"Father, I'm right here!" Mahina screamed.

Without any indication that he heard, he closed his eyes, uttered a death gurgle and became unresponsive.

Mahina shrieked and fell across his body, which already felt as cold as ice. Her pain was overwhelming, and she thought her heart might explode.

Why wasn't I here for him? she asked herself.

Why?

The familiar voice returned. *Mahina, come back. You've experienced what you needed. Come back ... come back ...*

Gradually, Mahina could once again hear the sounds of the beach. When she opened her eyes, she discovered Tiare sitting in front of her, nodding her head in approval.

"Well done, sister," Tiare whispered. "Well done."

Teacher and student sat quietly, listening to the melody of the ocean.

Mahina quietly asked, "Please explain what just happened."

"Mahina, you just faced a dark part of yourself. I might suppose that you feel guilt, and maybe even shame, for leaving your family to fend for themselves as the difficult times for Rapa Nui approached. Is that not true?"

"Yes, it is."

"Your meditation allowed you to recognize it and gave you the opportunity to heal that painful place. You did hear me say that the scenes were not real, didn't you?"

"I did," Mahina sighed, a look of relief on her face. "But it was all so real."

"They were only symbolic of what your deepest fears were. We will meet again soon, but your practice for the time being is to spend much of your days in meditation. Let your dark places bubble up to the surface. Once your recognize them, you can breathe and send love to them. In this way, you can heal. Do you understand?"

Mahina felt her eyes fill with tears as she reviewed the events of her meditation. "I do."

Tiare leaned over and gently squeezed Mahina's shoulder. "Sister," she whispered, "the path of the shaman is not easy, nor should it be. Only a select few are able to walk the painful way. The time ahead will be the most agonizing you will have ever experienced, but I am confident you will be able to persevere. Remember, I will be here to support you."

Mahina openly wept. "Thank . . . you."

Tiare wrapped her arms around Mahina and looked to the sky. She closed her eyes for a moment, breathed in and out, and let her consciousness expand.

The evil is closer than I thought, she realized, as she felt a darkness tearing at the edges of her mind. *I must be vigilant.*

Tiare sighed and held Mahina tight.

Chapter 8

Daniel awoke early in his hotel, the Wellington, located in the heart of London. Dawn's light beamed through a gap in the olive-green, heavy velvet curtains. Daniel yawned and stretched his arms above his head, trying to shake off the jet lag.

Late last night on his mobile, he had received an e-mail from Gordon Green, instructing Daniel to meet him in front of the hotel at nine the following morning. From there, they would drive to Salisbury. Once they arrived at their destination, they would go to Stonehenge as the first stop on their itinerary.

Daniel was excited about seeing the ancient monument, but he was distracted by his concern for Mahina-and Tiare. Knowing Rapa Nui was in a time zone five hours later than London, he dared not phone last night, as it would have been three a.m. in Rapa Nui, and he knew he would have wakened her.

Instead, he chose to call this morning, but there was no answer. He supposed Mahina was working at the school, but he was eager to hear her voice. Mahina was a master of the ancient *rongorongo* script—she had learned it first hand—but was still in the process of learning to read and write the Rapanui language, so texting her was not an option. He would try to speak with her this evening. As always, in Rapanui, the language they both spoke. He would one day teach her English, but not now.

Since her arrival in modern society, every day was filled with challenges. She had to learn to use a telephone, understand electrical appliances, drive a car, comprehend the monetary system and adjust to new foods... no, learning English could come later.

Right now she needs all of her attention focused on becoming Tiare's successor

After a quick breakfast of poached eggs, buttered toast with strawberry jam, and, of course, English Breakfast Tea, he shouldered his backpack, pulled his suitcase behind him and headed out of the hotel into the foggy, brisk February air. Daniel shuddered as the biting weather penetrated his usually warm, fleece-lined jacket.

After a short wait on the bustling street, Daniel was greeted by a dapper gentleman who held a sign with *Fishinghawk* written on it in elegant script. The man appeared to be in his early fifties and wore a nicely-fitted green tweed three-piece suit covered by an open black trench coat. From his vest pocket hung the gold chain of a pocket watch. He was tall and slender, and had dark red hair with a darker moustache. His bushy eyebrows closely matched the color of his hair.

"Chief Inspector Gordon Green?" Daniel asked.

"Right," he said, as he extended his hand. "And you must be the famous Hawk?"

Daniel shook it. "Well, I'm not sure how famous I am. Nice to meet you, Chief Inspector."

"Oh, you're the talk of the town around here. The way you solved that series of murders on Easter Island was bloody brilliant."

"Thank you," Daniel said. "But you have to understand that I had a lot of help on those cases." He thought of his grandpa and parents. "I couldn't have done it by myself."

"I say, we need all the guidance we can get with the murders here. We are in a bloody shambles. And that's why we've called you in."

Green pulled his watch from his pocket and glanced at it. "But, for now, let's chivvy along; we've got a schedule to keep." He led Daniel to an unmarked black car, parked in front of the hotel.

"Allow me, I will put your bag in the boot," Green said, as he took Daniel's suitcase and put it in the trunk. After slamming it shut, Daniel and the British inspector took their places in the back seat.

"First, let me introduce our driver. Hawk, I'd like you to meet Inspector Davies."

Davies turned and nodded to Daniel, politely saying, "Sir." His face was thin and clean shaven, and he looked to be in his late twenties, somewhere close to Daniel's age. His hair was blonde and close-cropped.

Daniel nodded back in recognition. "Nice to meet you, Inspector."

Green added, "Inspector Davies is new to the force, and he will drive us to Stonehenge. Scotland Yard requires his presence in London this evening, so I have arranged for another driver in Salisbury, a local chap who has fallen on some hard times over the past few years. I've offered him this job as a way of helping him out."

"Very good."

Davies turned his attention on pulling out onto the busy street. Pedestrians moved past the car, intent on finding their way to work in the frenzied morning traffic. The looks on their faces varied from serious to angry, any signs of happiness being conspicuously absent.

To Daniel, everything about London seemed crowded, noisy and busy, and he felt like a bee trapped in the middle of a hive. He longed for the quiet countryside of Rapa Nui.

As the car moved into the maelstrom, Green said, "First, I'd like to let you know a bit about me. I was raised in Salisbury and have been in the detective service for around twenty-five years. Before I began police work, I was a history major at Oxford, and I wrote my thesis on Stonehenge. All things historical—especially topics that are unusual or mysterious—are of interest to me."

"So, should I call you *Professor* Green?"

"Of course not," Green flashed an embarrassed smile and cleared his throat. "If you wish a title for me, I prefer Chief Inspector. I love history, but I learned long ago that my interests and talents were more in line with criminal investigations than with bygone times."

"We'll talk more about Stonehenge later. For now, let's go over the murders. I want you to be as up-to-date as possible regarding your reasons for being here. We have a couple of hours of travel time, and privacy may be an issue later."

"Good."

"Remember when I first talked with you, and I told you there were four victims?"

"Yes."

"Forgive me for not telling you in my e-mail, but I preferred to tell you in person. As of two days ago, there is a fifth."

"Oh, no."

"It's true. Since the murders began at Stonehenge, we'll go there first. After that I'd like to take you to the home where the latest victim was murdered. The iron isn't exactly hot, but it's still lukewarm, and perhaps you'll come up with something that we at Scotland Yard have missed. But, for now, I'd like to go through the list of those killed. Sound good?"

Daniel nodded.

"The first victim was a guard at Stonehenge: his name was Oliver Hamilton. He was a retired constable from Salisbury, in his early seventies, and he worked from dusk 'til dawn, five nights a week, to supplement his retirement income. He thought employment at Stonehenge would help bring in some extra pounds to cover his budget. Little did he know that someone was willing to kill him to have one of the Stonehenge bluestones."

"Nothing is ever as easy as it seems to be," Daniel commented.

"Agreed. The second was a middle-aged woman, Penny Pumpernickel, owner of a local tea shop, who, as I mentioned, was killed four months ago. She originally moved here some twenty years ago from Edinburgh, Scotland.

"The third was a local chap, Edward Kingsley, sixty-four years old, who was born and raised in Salisbury. He was a highly respected librarian and the president of the Salisbury Chess Club. Rumor had it that he was next in line to be the Grandmaster of England, the highest title a chess player can attain."

"Sounds like an interesting man."

"Quite. The fourth was a woman from Sweden, Lovisa Lundberg. She was fifty-three, a schoolteacher who taught foreign languages at a secondary school—what you Americans call high school—in Salisbury. She was fluent in five languages, English, French, Swedish, German and Arabic. She moved here fifteen years ago.

"Now, the last one, Jacques Girard, was from Bordeaux, France, sixty-one years old, and was killed only two days ago. He moved here seventeen years ago—"

Daniel interrupted, "Don't you think it's a bit unusual that three of the five were from out of the country, and that they moved to Salisbury over a five year span?"

"We looked into it and believe it is just coincidence. We went over and over the dossiers of each of the victims and can find no connection that would indicate why they all moved here during that period."

"I see," Daniel said, warily, narrowing his eyes. He was not convinced and made a mental note to explore it further.

"Anyway, about Gerard: He was a sommelier of renown and a French chef. His desserts, especially his tarte Tatin, were felt by local culinary experts to be the best in the world."

"Tarte Tatin?"

"It's quite a smashing end to a meal, an upside-down tart in which the fruit, usually apples, are caramelized in butter and sugar before being cooked. I happened to have a slice at Jacques' restaurant, Chez Paris, the night before he died, and I was gobsmacked by the flavor."

"Gobsmacked?"

Green laughed out loud, then managed to say, "Amazed."

"I see," Daniel replied, slightly uncomfortable for not knowing these British idioms. "Did you happen to see the victim that night?"

"I did. Jacques had a routine of coming out of the kitchen and greeting his guests. His wife was in attendance, and he seemed unusually cheery. I had made it a habit of taking my wife Emma on the train from London to dine at his restaurant twice a year—yes, it was that good—and never have I seen him so chipper. It was as though he had received some very good news. I suppose we'll never know now, eh?"

"I guess not."

Green continued. "Our computers are running night and day to discover any common thread to these killings. Of course, you know about the large, empty safes that were in each of their houses, all scrubbed down by the killer, right?"

"Right."

"These safes were all high quality, but not as good as ones you might find, say, at a bank. They would have presented some difficulty to crack, but anyone who had taken an advanced locksmith course would have had no trouble with them. My guess is that secrecy was our victims' main defense, and none expected to be discovered."

"Fair enough."

"Other than that, we've only been able to come up with three things. First, except for Gerard, who had been married a little over thirty-five years, all were loners and had no committed romantic connections. Second, married or not, for at least five days of the week, all disappeared at some time during the day. Neighbors would sometimes see them return to their homes late at night, often after midnight—"

"And the last?" Daniel sounded curt, and he hadn't intended to.

"The most unusual discovery of all. Close examination of their past histories revealed that our victims, except for the guard at Stonehenge, were all of superior intelligence. Their IQ records placed each in the top five percent of the population—not a lout in the whole group. It's as if the killer were trying to take out the intelligentsia of Salisbury."

"Odd."

"Indeed. I know I've given you a lot to chew on, and I believe you're likely tired from your travels. I was awake most of the night trying to resolve a threat to the Queen. Most are groundless, but we always take seriously any problem related to the Royal Family. What do you say that we take a little kip?"

"Kip?"

"Nap. And we'll talk more about Stonehenge when we get there. I will join you. I am whacked."

"Sounds good to me," Daniel replied. He relaxed in his seat.

Green laid his head back, and in moments he was softly snoring.

Daniel realized how much he was already enjoying getting to know the multi-faceted Chief Inspector. *I will need to trust my British colleague's background in history and attention to detail.* He knew both would serve them well as they probed deeply into this puzzling series of murders.

Daniel settled back and watched the scenery gradually change as their car traveled from the heart of London into the countryside. To his delight, the quaintness and order of the cultivated fields reminded him of his home state, Oklahoma.

Now, though, in preparation for this case, Daniel could feel his ordinarily fine-tuned intuition going into overdrive. He could appreciate the faint hint of coffee wafting back from the front seat—no doubt the drink Davies had for breakfast. He noticed a slight stain of fresh black shoe polish under Green's brown leather shoes, certainly from someone who sat there recently, one who wished to make a good impression. Out of the window, he saw a rabbit dive into its hole as the car passed by.

His perceptions accelerated, and he felt his consciousness expand.

I'm ready—for whatever comes my way.

For now, however, Daniel knew he needed to rest. As he closed his eyes and leaned against the car window, Daniel discovered he was unable to quiet his active mind. Questions repetitively rolled through his awareness:

Why kill someone for a bluestone?

What was the connection between the murder at Stonehenge and the ones in Salisbury?

Daniel had no idea.

Chapter 9

Mahina and Tiare sat facing each other on the floor in the depths of a hidden cavern near Ahu Akivi, an inland collection of seven aged, well-preserved *moai*. A white candle, one that Tiare had earlier set on the ground in front of them, emitted a soft, still light. A black canvas tote bag lay at Tiare's side.

Using a flashlight, Tiare had guided them far into the cavern's depths. Mahina noted that it was not like the narrow time cave she and Daniel had traversed last year. Rather, it was large and expansive, and she and Tiare could easily walk upright a great distance into the earth. Except for the hypnotic *plops* of water dripping from the ceiling of the cave into pools of water on the floor, there was dead silence. The cool, cave air refreshed them, and an occasional brown spider scurried by, attracted by the light.

Tiare clicked off her flashlight and stared at the candle. She whispered, "I love this place."

Mahina replied, "I do too. There's something meditative and peaceful about it."

"I agree. My shaman father, Tuki Vaka, used to bring me here for my training. I couldn't think of a better place to take you."

Even in the darkness of the cave, Tiare had appreciated the dark circles under Mahina's eyes and the stressed look on her face.

"Tell me, how are your meditations going?"

"Agonizingly," Mahina admitted, with a slight quiver in her voice. "I never realized how many dark places I had inside me. I feel like I'm about to go out of my mind."

"That is perfectly normal," Tiare said. "I began my training as a child, but still had plenty to work on. Since you are beginning your training at an older age, there will be much more for you to discover and heal."

" I'm not going crazy?"

"No, you're not going crazy," Tiare reassured her. "And, with time, your suffering will decrease, of that I am certain."

"That is good to know; I am glad it won't last forever. But before we continue, may I ask a question?"

"Of course."

"I'd like to understand more about Roberto Ika. There's something sweet and gentle about him, yet it seems that his mind does not function properly. I remember back in old Rapa Nui, how some were affected in this way. How is it that certain ones have such a disability?"

Tiare said, "That is an excellent question. I see that, as your meditations have drawn you close to the veil that separates sanity and insanity, you find yourself curious. Am I right?"

Mahina shuddered. "Yes, teacher."

"Very well, then. To answer your question, I must first ask you one. Do you believe that you live one, or more than one life?"

"My intuition tells me that I have walked the soil of this Earth many times, and I will do so many more times."

"Well spoken, my apprentice, and I agree with you. Reincarnation is not a usual tenet of shamanism, yet many of us who have penetrated the world of spirit view it as fact, rather than philosophical belief.

"So, to answer your question, it is hard to know the reason why some have an altered view of reality. There are many possible explanations, and I will go through but a few. First, you should know that all of us have a protective web—some call it the etheric web—that acts as a filter and separates our consciousness from other realities, other planes of existence. As long as it remains intact, you will be protected from their energies.

"This web can gradually be dissolved through different spiritual practices—especially deep meditation—and one can safely be exposed to the inner worlds when ready. The web can be temporarily damaged, though, by extreme emotional upheaval, such as fear, anger and shock. Such injury can also occur with the use of either hallucinogenic drugs or excessive intake of alcohol. If this happens, experiences and visions can arise for which one is not prepared, and that unfortunate person can have a difficult time discerning what is and is not reality.

"How hard that must be," Mahina sympathized.

"Certainly, there are other reasons, spiritual ones, that might cause one to be insane. It is possible insanity could be due to karma, in other words, your 'reward' for a misstep in a previous lifetime. But one can have good karma too and be given an active, healthy body and mind, due to beneficial actions that have been performed in lifetimes previously."

"I see."

"But I don't think it is as straightforward as that. I believe it is possible that some advanced souls may *choose* to have a physical or mental handicap."

"Why would they do that?" asked Mahina, a puzzled look on her face.

"It's all about growth. The harder the experience, the greater the opportunity they have for spiritual development. And this growth can occur, not only for the person, but also for those who interact with them, whether family, friends or adversaries." Tiare paused for a moment to let her words sink in.

"Now, about Roberto Ika. I have thought much about him and his situation over the years, and I now believe he is a very old and wise soul who has consciously chosen this pathway, not only for his growth but also the betterment of all. Quite a strong spirit is required to take on such a disability, and I think he's done an amazingly good job of managing it. Certainly, I'm a better person because I know him."

"Thank you, teacher." Mahina gently touched Tiare's shoulder. "I'm beginning to understand."

"Good." Tiare readjusted her legs, straightened her back and said, "Let us begin our work. As I told you, my father often brought me here for my preparation to be a shaman. The first time, though, he gave me instructions for a most sacred ritual: finding my animal guide. And that is your task for today. Have you fasted, as I have asked?"

"Yes. I have had nothing but water for the past twenty-four hours."

"Good. This will quicken your senses and make you more aware of the designs of spirit."

Tiare looked compassionately at her. "In a moment, I will depart. I will leave a blanket, several bottles of water, extra candles, matches and a flashlight for you to find your way out when your labor is done. I expect you will find the answers you seek within a few days. Please come to my home when you are finished. If I don't hear from you in forty-eight hours, I will be back to check on you. Do you understand?"

"Yes, teacher."

"A few final words: Mahina, our shamanic forebears saw animal guides as companions, teachers and spiritual advisors. If we ask, they can help us understand the mysteries of Earth that we humans often have a difficult time comprehending. Besides, with such a helper, you will never lose your pathway through the dream-like land of spirit. I hope that during this time you will discover your animal guide.

"Now, please close your eyes for a short prayer, the same one my father gave me in this cave so many years ago."

Tiare took a deep breath and felt a surge of emotion with the memory. She loved her father as much as anyone could. She closed her own eyes and intensely whispered:

> The sacred steps you take
>
> Have been walked before by your ancestors
>
> Tread mindfully and in silence
>
> Listen carefully
>
> Be aware
>
> Wisdom awaits you

Tiare lightly touched Mahina's cheek before standing. "I will be supportive of you, but this is a journey you must take by yourself."

After she emptied the promised articles from the canvas bag, Tiare said, "Goodbye, sister. May Spirit walk with you."

"Goodbye."

Tiare clicked on her flashlight and slowly, meditatively, strolled away.

Soon, Mahina could no longer hear her footsteps and the light faded.

She was alone.

At least, she thought she was.

Chapter 10

Daniel stared in astonishment. Standing before him was one of the most amazing things he had ever seen:

Stonehenge.

Granted, the *moai* and *ahus* on Easter Island were stunning. But this prehistoric grouping of stones had a unique, ancient energy about it, one he had never experienced before.

The flat surroundings and a thin layer of sparkling snow, which had the appearance of powdered sugar, accentuated even more the starkness of the formation. The air was cold, crisp and odorless, and a number of black-colored birds pecked around the small tufts of dead grass that protruded through the snow. Daniel identified three different species: jackdaws, rooks and crows. In the distance, he could see skylarks soaring high, singing over their territory.

Daniel and Green stood looking from the asphalt walkway in front of Stonehenge. A large crowd had gathered, even though it was the dead of winter. Daniel couldn't avert his eyes from it. It was entrancing, magnetizing, much like the glowing embers of a campfire. The varied calls of the birds only added to the mystique.

Green asked, as he stared at the sacred monument, "Hawk, what do you know about Stonehenge?"

"Not as much as I would like."

Green nodded his head. "Okay, let me give you some background you will find interesting. You see, historians tell us that Stonehenge has been used as a temple, a place of burial, celebration and ceremony."

"When was its construction begun?"

"Around three thousand BC."

"Not BCE?"

"No," Green answered. "Here in the UK we use BC and AD, not BCE, which stands for Before the Common Era, or CE, which stands for Common Era."

"Understood."

"The first Stonehenge was a simple circular ditch and bank, about one hundred and ten meters in diameter, which was dug out by people wielding red deer antlers and picks."

Daniel asked, "What was its primary function then?"

"We are not certain, but the so-named Aubrey Holes, fifty-six circular pits, four to five meters apart and placed just inside the inner edge of the bank, were originally believed to have wooden posts or stone pillars in them. Researchers later discovered that these holes were filled with cremated human bones. So, historians believe, in its early years, Stonehenge was likely a cemetery."

"Interesting."

"Truly. Around twenty-five hundred BC, the stones began to arrive. The stone lying down at the entry to the formation is the Slaughter Stone I was telling you about, the stone on which the slain guard was found. See the larger stones on the outside circle?"

Daniel peered at the formation. "I do."

"They are known as sarsens. Originally, there were thirty of them, though now there are only seventeen. You notice that some have stones connecting them on the top?"

At last, something I know. "Lintels?"

"Yes, lintels, very good." Green looked pleased. "They're locked together by tongue-and-groove joints on the vertical faces, and mortise-and-tenon joints on the horizontal. Moving inward, the next setting of sarsens is a massive horseshoe of stones, some that weigh over forty tons. The sarsens came from an area some thirty kilometers away called Marlborough Downs.

"The smaller stones—the bluestones—form a concentric circle just inside the outside sarsens, and an inner horseshoe of pillars just inside the sarsen horseshoe. I know you can't tell from here, but the stolen bluestone was taken from the outer ring. In a moment, we'll have a closer look."

Daniel couldn't wait. "Good."

"Now, the bluestones can weigh as much as three tons each—"

Daniel interrupted, "So moving equipment must have been used to haul away the one that was stolen?"

"Precisely. In the dark of night, with the guard out of the way and no one else around, heavy duty machinery was brought in to move it. In case you didn't know, the bluestones originate from the Preseli Hills in Wales, over two hundred forty kilometers to the west."

Daniel asked, "How could an ancient people move such large stones?"

"Not with the help of aliens, I assure you," Green sardonically answered. "Like the statues on Easter Island and the Egyptian pyramid stones, some crackpots have postulated that the sarsens and bluestones of Stonehenge were moved by extraterrestrials. Isn't it odd how, when people run across events they can't explain, they decide it must have been ETs that were behind it all?"

Green smiled a toothy grin, and Daniel chuckled.

Green went on, "From Marlborough Downs, the huge sarsens were likely dragged on a wooden sledge running on rails. This would require around two hundred men and would take an estimated twelve days.

"The bluestones would have first been transported by land, then likely by sea up to the mouth of the river Avon, which is close to Stonehenge."

Green turned as he said, "Now, if you'll look to the left, toward the Slaughter Stone, you'll see the end of the Avenue—"

"The Avenue?"

"Yes, the Avenue. This begins on the bank of the River Avon, around two and a half kilometers away, and ends here at Stonehenge. Some believe the Avenue was the ceremonial way for pilgrims to approach Stonehenge."

"What kind of ceremonies?"

"Your guess is as good as mine. Now, besides being a cemetery, Stonehenge was constructed so its axis is in alignment with the yearly movements of the sun. On the longest day of the year, the summer solstice, June twenty-first, the sun rises in the northeast, and its first rays beam into the center of Stonehenge. On the shortest day of the year, the winter solstice, December twenty-first, the light from sunset shines into the heart of Stonehenge from the opposite side, the southwest."

"Fascinating."

"Indeed. So, it seems probable that Stonehenge was built to celebrate not only the longest day of the year, but also the shortest."

Daniel was puzzled. "Let's go back to the bluestones. Why would an early civilization go to so much trouble to transport them such a great distance? It seems that there must have been stones of a similar size a lot closer."

Gordon whispered as if he were sharing a secret. "Hawk, that is the most important question of all. There are some, including me, who believe there was a specific purpose for transporting these stones from so far away. Have you ever seen a bluestone up close before?"

"No, I haven't."

"They are gorgeous," Green said, breathlessly. "In many ways, cross sections of the stones have the appearance of a starry nighttime sky. Some stones have a blue-green or blue-gray appearance and are dotted with white spots, which look much like stars. Many folk tales from Wales exist about the healing power of bluestones, stories that may have their origins from prehistoric times. A famous poem—one I have memorized—was written by Layamon, a precursor of Chaucer, about Stonehenge in twelve fifteen AD."

Green had a faraway look in his eyes as he recited:

> The stones are great;
> And magic power they have;
> Men that are sick;
> Fare to that stone;
> And they wash that stone;
> And with that water bathe away their illness.

"And that was the topic of my thesis. I believe Stonehenge was more than what historians say. I maintain that it was also a place of healing."

Daniel said, "I've never heard this theory before."

"The idea is not discussed much, and I was laughed at by my colleagues when I presented my research. But, in two thousand eight this hypothesis was reintroduced by archaeologists Darvill and Wainwright. They added as evidence the remains of a wealthy man, between thirty-five and forty-five years of age. He was called the Amesbury Archer, and his carcass was discovered about eight kilometers from Stonehenge. He was terribly ill from an infected kneecap and an abscessed tooth that had eroded away part of his jaw. He had traveled from the Swiss or German Alps, and it seems likely that he came to Stonehenge in hope of being healed."

"How intriguing this theory is."

"Undeniably." Green had a twinkle in his eyes.

"To finish with the history of Stonehenge, its construction took more than one thousand years, and it was essentially finished by sixteen hundred BC. No one knows how long it continued to be used as a living temple, though we are certain that period concluded well before the Roman conquest of forty-three AD. Well, I've told you a lot of bloody information in a short period of time. Do you have any queries?"

"Yes. Some have said that the Druids were involved in the building of Stonehenge."

Green chuckled before he answered, "Crikey, Hawk, that idea is a real clanger. The Druids were Iron Age priests who appeared over a thousand years after Stonehenge was abandoned. They had nothing to do with the construction of Stonehenge, much as I'm sure they would like to take credit for it."

Embarrassed, Daniel said nothing.

"Enough jabbering," Green concluded, "I've arranged for us to walk among the stones, if you'd like."

"There's nothing I'd enjoy more."

Five thousand years of history loomed before him as he and Green were allowed to enter the central area.

Daniel was flooded with powerful emotions as he walked through and around the stones. He noticed a deep indentation in the soil where the stolen bluestone once stood, and from the entryway up to it were areas of denuded soil—no doubt places that had been raked over to hide the marks made by the moving equipment.

Daniel's head swam with the peculiarity of it all.

Why?

Chapter 11

The dark force uncurled from its shadowy, murky corner deep in the earth, not far from where Mahina sat, in a place where no human could walk or crawl to. The presence preferred concealed locations where there was little, if any light. Brightness caused excruciating pain for him.

He wafted out from his secluded nook and, after maneuvering through a number of connecting crevices, oozed out of a crack in the damp wall of the rock-lined cave and hovered above the meditating Mahina, wondering whether or not this was the right moment to strike.

He carefully pondered his decision. At first glance, all seemed easy enough. The aged shaman, the strong one—the one who he could not overcome—had left. He knew Mahina had not yet developed her full spiritual capabilities, but her inner core was vibrant and full of strength. Even though She was young and inexperienced as a shaman, besting her would be no easy task, especially if the old woman sensed her difficulty and returned.

No, now was not the time to fall upon the younger woman. He had spent much time dabbling in the dark arts in a forbidden, evil place, where most would be afraid to go, and had formulated a plan of attack. Without a doubt, he knew he must weaken the older woman first.

And so, he proceeded. He prayed a wicked prayer, one burned into his memory:

> 'O Lono
> Listen to my voice,
> This is the plan
> Rush upon Tiare Rapu and enter
> Enter and curl up
> Curl up and straighten out

He felt the power of the hex erupt from him. Tiare would soon be as docile and as helpless as a lamb, and, when she was incapacitated, he would exact as much pain on the younger one as he could. He would engulf and absorb her in his darkness. He anticipated the ecstasy of hearing her scream in agony.

Nothing would make him happier.

Just after Tiare left, Mahina sat on the floor of the cave with her eyes closed, sensing, rather than seeing the still light of the candle. All at once, with her spiritual senses, she perceived an ice-cold, prickly sensation floating just above her. Following her meditative practice, she kept her eyes closed and directed her mind upward to explore the odd phenomenon, which abruptly disappeared.

What is it? she wondered.

Not to be distracted further, Mahina opened her eyes and watched the candle, wishing her mind to be as motionless as the flame. She closed her eyes again, visualizing the candle in her mind.

Minutes passed to hours as she held the image firmly. Thoughts randomly presented themselves, over and over again. She breathed with them, and their power over her gradually diminished.

She then reached down and picked up two pieces of obsidian from the ground where she had placed them earlier. She held them in front of her and clicked them together in rhythm, timing her breathing with the sound. She felt herself entering an altered state of consciousness.

As she touched the rocks together, she chanted a verse, one which had been taught to her by her father, Hotu Iti:

> Ancient guides, from the rising and setting of the sun
> Where earth and sky merge at the horizon

> Ancient guides, rearward tilting, frontwards bending
> On the right side of the sky
> Inhaling and exhaling in the sky
> Whispering in the sky
> Vibrating in the sky
> Hastening in the sky
> I am your descendant
> Protect me!

A feeling of warmth spread over her. She opened her heart and mind, waiting for the sounds and images of animals, looking for one that stood out to her, one that seemed significant.

Her vision began in the sea. She visualized a beautiful blue whale, cavorting in the ocean and leaping with joy out of the sea, water spewing from its spout. Then, with her spiritual sight, she looked under the water and saw pods of dolphins swimming in formation in its depths, bobbing their noses as they caught squirming fish.

Mahina was next drawn to the land, where she saw a number of small lizards of various colors scurrying across the black, volcanic soil of Rapa Nui. They darted back and forth, alert and active.

In her altered state, she felt a generalized tingling and a had a feeling of anticipation. She refocused her mind and listened intently to her inner ear.

Before long, Mahina heard the flapping of wings, then a large, beautiful white bird flew in front of her and landed. A black feathered stripe arose from both corners of its mouth, which extended to and around its eyes. Its bill was bright red and curved downward, and a single long red plume extended about twenty inches from its white tail feathers.

Mahina instantly recognized it to be a red-tailed tropicbird, known to her people as a *tavake*. Even in her meditative state, she melted into tears.

Tavake was the name of her long-dead mother.

Regaining her composure, Mahina mentally whispered softly to the bird, *Are you my animal guide?*

I am, as the bird cocked its head.

Mahina heard these unspoken words in her head and asked, *Are you my mother?*

No, but I will care for you and love you much as a mother would.

Then answer my question: What was that cold feeling I experienced a little earlier?

An evil that wishes you harm.

What can I do about it?

Nothing for the moment. Follow your pathway, and if you listen, answers will come to you.

But I must know more...

For you to fully experience the growth that is necessary, you must discover the answers by yourself. Remember, all solutions to any questions already exist inside you.

I understand.

The *tavake* then took flight, its bright red plume bobbing as it rose swiftly into the air.

Tears of joy streamed down her face as Mahina opened her eyes to a pitch black cave. She groped into the void in front of her and touched what remained of the candle. The ashes were cold; the candle had burned out long ago.

She smiled against the darkness and felt a sense of relief and triumph. She found what she had sought.

Mahina wiped her eyes with her sleeve, reached to the cold cave floor and felt the flashlight lying by her feet. She switched it on, gathered her belongings and began the long walk back to Tiare's home. She was tired, hungry and, at the same time, exhilarated.

A major step had been accomplished.

Tiare sat on the couch at her home, concerned and waiting for Mahina's return. She had detected an evil presence in the cave as she left but decided against going back. Somehow, she knew the time for an attack had not yet come; though, if it did, she would sense it and would return to Mahina's side—immediately.

But when would it? she wondered.

At that moment, she felt tingling and numbness to both of her feet. It slowly moved up to her legs. She quickly probed the odd sensation with her inner eye and realized that it was not created by a physical cause but, rather, the result of dark magic.

She was still able to walk, so she dashed over to her chest of herbs, pulled from one of the drawers a necklace of ti leaves, and placed it around her neck. She found a fan made of the same leaves and cooled her perspiring face with it. Her actions slowed the creeping movement up her legs, but it did not go away.

With dismay, Tiare realized she had been foolish. The evil hex she was experiencing could have been prevented by simply planting ti at the corners of her home. She would make sure it was put in the ground around Mahina and Daniel's house tomorrow.

Too late, Tiare knew that she had underestimated her dark foe. Never would she have guessed that he—yes, she sensed her opponent was masculine—would have been willing to take such a risk to obtain this magic.

Tiare knew exactly what she was dealing with.

An evil of great power.

The Death Prayer.

Chapter 12

Daniel and Detective Green sat in pensive silence as they were driven away from Stonehenge. After having roamed for well over an hour through the ancient ruins, Daniel felt completely overwhelmed by the feelings he had. No words could describe them.

Daniel wished Mahina could have seen it with him, remembering her reaction to the images of Stonehenge she had viewed on his computer. Tonight, he planned to chat with her. He didn't care what time it was in Rapa Nui.

Their driver sat sullenly in the front and didn't say a word to either of them. He sported a black-and-white herringbone flat cap, and greasy, black hair hung loosely down to his shoulders. He was unshaven and wore a soiled dark-brown trench coat. The odor wafting from him into the back seat was one of cheap wine.

Green broke the silence. "Hawk, we should be at Girard's home soon. Until then, let's take care of business. You'll be staying, until this is all said and done, at the Salisbury Bed and Breakfast. It's close to downtown, and the owners, James and Emily Trueblood, have lived in Salisbury most of their lives and will help you in any way they can. Besides, their breakfasts are the finest in the area, and they make the best blood pudding—"

"*Blood* pudding?"

"Oh, yes." Green's bushy eyebrows raised. "Blood pudding. It's actually a type of sausage made with animal blood. It also has grain, usually oats, mixed in with it. You should give it a go—it's not as bad as it sounds."

Daniel cringed. "I think I'll pass."

Green still had a smirk on his face as he said, "Tonight I'm headed back to London. We have not made any progress on the death threat to the Queen, and everyone available is being called in to work the situation. I'll have my mobile phone with me if you need to ring."

"How do I get around?" Daniel hoped it wouldn't be the disheveled man who drove the car.

"No problem. Ned, your driver, lives here in town and will be available at any time to take you wherever you need to go. Right, Ned?"

Ned turned around, stared at them with shifty bloodshot eyes and nodded.

"Watch the road!" Green bellowed.

Ned quickly turned back around, swerved sharply to avoid an oncoming vehicle and grumbled, "As you say, guv'nuh."

Daniel flinched with his near-death experience, then he took a few deep breaths and asked, "Where do you recommend I begin?"

"That, I will leave up to you. I've heard all about your intuition from Chief Kelly at the NYPD, and I might guess that you'll figure out where you want to begin to sniff out this case."

After a short drive, they pulled up in front of a spacious, two-story home on an oversized lot. Even though the evening was growing late, Daniel could see that the trees were large, barren English oaks, and evergreen shrubs surrounded the black antique brick building. Several white British police cars, with markings in royal blue and light green, were parked in front.

"Was Girard wealthy?" asked Daniel.

"Absolutely," Green confirmed. "He brought buckets of money with him from Paris. His father, who managed one of the finest casinos in Monaco, left him a huge inheritance."

Green and Daniel exited the car into the frosty air and walked up to the front door. They were greeted by a stocky man who was dressed in a gray suit covered by a darker gray overcoat. He was a mirror image of Teddy Roosevelt; the only thing missing was a monocle.

"Inspector Fishinghawk, I'd like you to meet Inspector Edward DeWoody. He's the local detective in charge of the investigation."

DeWoody extended his hand. "Jolly good to meet you, Mr. Fishinghawk. I'm glad you decided to give your British allies a hand with this sordid affair."

Daniel shook it. "I'm glad to be of service."

DeWoody added, "We have promised Mrs. Girard we would be out of the house by this evening, so we're expecting her at any time. We've got things pretty well wrapped up anyway. Would you like to have a look at the place?"

Daniel nodded and followed DeWoody as he opened the heavy, wooden front door, and they entered the home. A large, sparkling crystal chandelier hung in the entryway, and a stunning painting of brightly colored water lilies decorated the opposite wall. Daniel searched his eidetic memory. The style closely matched that of the French impressionist Claude Monet, but he had never seen this particular work in any art book.

DeWoody observed Daniel's stare and said, "What you're looking at is an original Monet, and the security system to protect it is top notch—the best money can buy."

"Why didn't the murderer steal that?"

"We're not sure. Must have been focused on what was in the safe."

Daniel asked, "How did the killer break in without being caught? Surely there were surveillance cameras? The painting alone would warrant them."

"Cameras circle the property, but Girard had switched them off earlier. Why, we don't know. He was by himself when the murder occurred. As you can see, the front door is as solid as a rock, and there is a peephole that Girard was able to look through. Girard opened the door for his murderer, and we can only guess that he knew him. Was it someone whose identity he wished to shield? We'll never know now. Of the other murders that have occurred in town, the only one where there was a break in was at the tea shop of Penny Pumpernickel."

"I see," Daniel said, wrinkling his forehead in thought.

DeWoody went on. "Girard was shot dead when the killer entered, and forensics has confirmed that it's the same weapon used in all of the other murders. A veritable lake of blood pooled on the floor that's taken every bit of these two days to get cleaned up."

Daniel glanced at the white baseboard. A line of a dark maroon stained the bottom of it.

Good luck getting that out, he thought.

"Now, if you'll follow me," DeWoody continued, "let's go down into the wine cellar, the location of the safe." He walked around the corner, into the dining area, then down an ornate, spiral wrought-iron stairway. Daniel and Green followed close behind.

Daniel scanned the room. The dimly lit space was like something out of a movie. He felt like he was in a cave, and nearly every inch of space of the walls was filled with wooden racks and bins full of dusty bottles of wine. To his left, the room extended deep into darkness, so much so that Daniel was unable to see the far wall. He guessed there had to be thousands of bottles.

A thermostat and humidifier controls sat mounted on the wall to his right. *With this vast collection*, Daniel reasoned, *the conditions would have to be kept near perfect.*

Daniel looked around. "Where's the safe?"

DeWoody said, "Mr. Fishinghawk..."

"Please call me Hawk."

DeWoody nodded. "Hawk, we never would have found the safe if the murderer hadn't left the concealing wall open. Look here."

He walked over to a bin, reached under it and clicked a hidden latch. Daniel held his breath as one of the walls of wine creaked open, revealing a huge safe, the door of which was partially ajar.

DeWoody opened it wide. "As you can see, it's completely empty. Did Green tell you that all of the safes of those murdered had been scrubbed clean of any residue?"

"He did."

"Well, in this safe, our murderer didn't quite get it all. There was a tiny bit of dust in one corner that the killer missed—"

"And?" Daniel interrupted..

"And under the microscope we were able to identify very small particles—of gold."

"Gold?"

"Yes, gold. For some reason, whoever killed and robbed Girard and our other Salisbury victims wanted no one to know what was stored in the safes."

"Strange," Daniel said. "Seems to me that one might *expect* to find gold in a safe. Why would keeping that a secret be so important to the murderer?"

"We haven't a clue," DeWoody confessed.

Daniel paused for a moment in thought, then asked, "Anything else stolen?"

"Not that we can tell."

Daniel walked over to the safe and stuck his head inside it. He took a slow, deep breath through his nose. "What's that odor?"

Green also strolled up to the safe and, along with DeWoody, inhaled deeply.

"I can't get a whiff of anything," Green said, inhaling and exhaling repeatedly.

"Nor can I," DeWoody confirmed.

Both looked expectantly at Daniel.

Daniel shrugged his shoulders. "It's a very faint scent . . . like a mixture of sulfur and vinegar. Very odd."

DeWoody added, "I say, Hawk, as you can tell, we've got our knickers in a twist over these murders. I'm not sure what—"

"Jacques! Oh, Jacques! I won't be able to live without you!" A woman screamed from upstairs, startling the group.

The three detectives dashed up the stairs to discover two women standing in the living area in front of an oil painting of a couple. The one wailing was a black haired and well-dressed middle aged woman, wearing a black business suit with a tight skirt that rested just above her knees. At her side was a shorter, younger woman with cropped, light brown hair, dressed in a similar dark brown outfit.

The younger one stroked the older one's shoulder. "Elisabeth," she consoled in a soothing voice, "you must calm yourself. Jacques would not wish you to act this way."

Elisabeth sobbed as she held a white tissue to her face. "But my Jacques is dead, sister! How can I be any other way? Monique, you should know that."

Daniel looked up at the painting. The lady pictured there was Elisabeth herself, a beautiful, stately woman, and he could only guess that the handsome man standing with her was her late husband, Jacques. The artistry of the painting was amazing and must have cost a fortune to have commissioned. But, for this couple, money was no object.

DeWoody cleared his throat, and the two women turned to face him.

"Ladies, I'm sorry to interrupt you, but I must let you know that we have finished our inspection of the home, and you can now live in it again, if you want."

Elisabeth Girard spun around to face DeWoody. "Of course I wish to live here.

I want to bathe myself forever in the memory of my late husband."

"Naturally," DeWoody said, with a warm look on his face. "Madame Girard, I'd like to take a moment to introduce you to our American colleague, one whom Scotland Yard has asked to help with the investigation, Inspector Daniel Fishinghawk."

"I'm glad to meet you," she said graciously, as she looked at him up and down.

Daniel noticed her makeup was perfectly applied, accentuating her features rather than hiding them. It was as if she were saying, *Why should I mask perfection?* She was stunningly attractive, and she knew it.

Daniel caught a glimmer of curiosity in her stare and had the feeling she was a bit of an enchantress. He had dealt with women in the past who, intentionally or unintentionally, flirted with him, and he had no interest in engaging her.

"Madame Girard, I know this is a very bad time for you, but would you mind if I asked you a few questions?"

"Of course you may not!" her sister loudly interrupted. "Since I arrived yesterday from my home in Nice, she has been interrogated by the police far too many times. I won't have any more of it."

"Monique," Elisabeth replied, in a lilting, seductive French accent, "*Merci*, but how can I refuse? Have you not been reading the newspaper? Detective Fishinghawk is the one who solved the brutal murders on Easter Island. He may be the best detective in the world, and I would give anything to have my husband's killer caught. *Non*, I will answer his questions. Gentlemen, my sister and I will sit on the couch, and you may take chairs across from us."

Elisabeth and Monique gracefully sat down on a white velvet couch covered with white fluffy cushions. While they rearranged the cushions and the detectives took their places, the scent of Chanel N°5 drifted into their faces from Elisabeth's side of the couch, reminding Daniel of the scent always liberally applied by the mayor's wife in New York City.

Daniel well remembered the words of Detective Chief Kip Kelly, after he and Kelly had met the mayor and his wife at a New York City police function. Kelly had rolled his eyes and quietly remarked, "That's Chanel Number Five that you smell, the perfume of the fucking rich and famous. My ex-wife soaked herself in it and, because of that, damn near bankrupted me. Every time I complained, she would say, 'Remember what Marilyn Monroe said when asked what she wore in bed—Chanel Number Five.'"

Repressing a grin and bringing his mind back to the present, Daniel refocused on Elisabeth as she reached down into a black Louis Vuitton handbag sitting on the walnut-stained wooden floor. She pulled out a cigarette, lit it and exhaled smoke over her right shoulder. One of the largest diamonds Daniel had ever seen glittered on her left ring finger.

She purred, "Detective Fishinghawk, what would you like to know?"

Stone-faced, Daniel asked, "Madame Girard, why did you and your husband move here from Paris some twenty years ago?"

"Opportunity, *Monsieur*, opportunity!"

"What do you mean by that?"

"My husband was the best chef in all of France." Her body posture straightened, proudly. "Jacques was the top of his class at Le Cordon Bleu and one of the most brilliant men I have ever met." She cast a hungry stare at Daniel.

"And you must know, *Monsieur*, that I am very fond of intelligent men."

Daniel ignored the innuendo. "Go on."

Not accustomed to having her advances brushed aside, she raised her chin haughtily. "Shortly after he graduated, the French team he was a member of won the Bocuse d'Or, one of the world's most prestigious cooking competitions.

"In his career, he was the head chef at many of Paris' finest restaurants, and, simply put, there was nothing more to accomplish in Paris, or France for that matter. We both felt that establishing a fine French restaurant elsewhere would let some other country know of my husband's extraordinary skills."

Daniel leaned forward. "Why Salisbury?"

"*Monsieur*, have you been here long?"

"No."

"Then you must not know that in the past this location lacked any first-class eating establishments. It was here we felt we had the greatest chance for success, especially considering the tourist population. Jacques was not afraid of competition, though, for in Paris he had already faced down many of the world's greatest chefs. Once we arrived here, my husband threw himself—how do you Americans say it?—headlong into his work. I rarely saw him at home."

Daniel said, "I understand. I'm sure you know that, of the three people killed who were not from Salisbury, all arrived here close to the same time. Did you or your husband know any of them—beforehand?"

"Of course not. What are you saying?"

Daniel squinted in concentration. "I'm wondering if there might be some kind of a connection, some shared reason for coming here."

"Not that I know of."

"Very good," Daniel said. "Another question: Do you know of anyone who might have had a motive to kill your husband?"

"Everyone loved my husband. He had no enemies."

"Did you know about the safe?"

A nervous look crossed her face. "I did not. A year or so ago, I made an extended trip to see my sister Monique in Nice. He must have had it placed in the basement then."

"Why?"

"Perhaps he wished to store valuables or papers there. I have no idea."

"Why do you think he never told you of it?"

Elisabeth shifted uncomfortably in her chair. "I do not know."

"Where were you at the time of your husband's death?"

A hint of anger flashed across her face. She quickly regained her composure and said, "I was in town, shopping with my sister."

Monique nodded.

Daniel leaned back in his chair. "I must assume that you've looked through the rest of your home."

"Yes, of course I did."

"Was anything else stolen?"

Daniel saw indecision on her face.

"Well..." Elisabeth slowly stammered. "I... I... don't think so."

All three inspectors leaned forward in their chairs. Something was amiss.

Daniel tersely said, "Please explain."

"Well, there is one place in our home that no one knows of. Its location is near the cellar where my husband stores his most valuable wines. It would be impossible for anyone to discover, so I didn't even bother to look there."

"How valuable?" Inspector DeWoody broke in.

"His most precious bottle is a nineteen eighty-five Henri Jayer Richebourg Grand Cru, Coits de Nuits, from France. It's worth upwards of twenty-five thousand American dollars. We've been saving it for our fiftieth wedding anniversary."

"May we see it?" Daniel stood and the other detectives joined him.

Elisabeth stared at him. "I don't like showing anyone our secret wine collection, but since you're the police, I will."

Everyone walked to the spiral staircase and began the walk down. When they arrived in the wine cellar, Madame Girard led them into the darkest part of the room. Daniel noticed her take her sister's hand.

"Watch your step," Elisabeth warned.

She reached into one of the nearby wine bins, flipped on a light switch and pulled out a small flashlight from a hidden niche.

Twenty steps later, at the end of the room, the group stopped before a bare wall. Even with the flashlight, the darkness threatened to swallow them up.

"Stand in front of the wall," Elisabeth gesticulated to the group and added, "Close together."

Once everyone had moved into position, she reached up then pulled down a chain close to the ceiling that was barely visible. A motor hummed, and the part of the floor they stood on began to sink like an elevator. It dropped into total darkness, and with a soft *thump* hit the floor of another room, this one much smaller.

"You can see why I wasn't worried about anyone finding this.," Elisabeth pointed the flashlight's beam of light to a wine rack that sat against the far wall. It held around twenty bottles.

"These are the best of the best," Elisabeth announced, with pride, as they approached.

Suddenly, she let out a soft gasp. "It can't be!"

"What?" Daniel began to scrutinize the rack and its bottles. She pointed the flashlight at an empty space toward the top of the rack. "The Henri Jayer Richebourg Grand Cru—it's gone!"

Daniel looked carefully at the floor to make sure he was not marring any evidence. It was apparent the killer had brushed it free of any footprints. Daniel cautiously approached.

He moved his face close to the empty spot. He inhaled deeply.
Just as I thought:
Vinegar and sulfur.

Chapter 13

"What is the Death Prayer?" Mahina anxiously asked, a slight tremor in her voice.

Tiare lay on the couch, a cool wet rag on her forehead, her feet elevated on two pillows. Mahina had never seen her look so pale.

Tiare spoke weakly, saying, "It's an ancient, dark magic that had its origins in Hawaii. Shamans there are called kahunas, and it has also been called the Kahuna Death Prayer."

"How does it work?"

"Using his powers, an evil shaman—and in my case it is a man,-enslaves from one to three discarnate spirits, and under hypnotic suggestion, they absorb some of the *mana*—vital force or power—of the shaman. Once that is accomplished, they follow the scent of their intended victim, using a bit of their prey's hair, blood or clothing."

"How did he get any of *that*?"

Tiare shrugged her shoulders and said, "I wish I knew."

"Once they find their prey, the spirits are instructed to 'curl up and straighten out,' which means they penetrate the victim's body and they begin to slowly extract their *mana*. That person would then have numbness that begins in the feet and gradually makes its way up to the heart. When it reaches the heart, the unfortunate one dies."

Mahina could barely catch her breath. "How long does this usually take?"

"Three days. But in my case, it will take much longer. I have embraced the protection of the ti leaves and my own personal healing energy."

"Can you cure yourself?"

"I will do all I can, but I have never dealt with a power such as this. I have confronted the spirits involved, but they are deeply controlled by the evil force, and I cannot convince them to leave me. Otherwise, I have no answers, but I will continue to search."

"Will Honu help you?"

"Honu is a blessed guide, yet she and I both know that, for my personal growth, I have to solve this problem without her assistance, even if I should die."

Mahina shook her head and pleaded, "What can I do to help you?"

"You have to continue to learn your shaman lessons, and we must accelerate your studies. If we look deeply, we might guess this experience will prove to be of benefit in your learning. I am certain that once I am incapacitated, the evil will strike at you. In my dreams I have learned that you are the primary target for this attack."

Mahina shuddered. "Who is this evil?"

"I have a guess, but I'm not ready to share my suspicions. The dark one has disguised his identity quite well."

Mahina openly wept and stood from her chair to embrace the old woman.

Tiare felt her heart open to Mahina, and she lovingly stroked her back.

Tiare resolutely thought: *I don't care if I'm ninety-five.*

I'm not ready to die.

Chapter 14

"The Death Prayer?"

"Yes, Dan-iel, the Death Prayer," Mahina confirmed.

Daniel had, at long last, been able to speak on the phone with his love. After visiting Girard's home, Ned had dropped him off at the bed and breakfast. The owners, James and Emily Trueblood, were out for the evening, and Daniel was checked into his second-story room by their employee, Lily, a vivacious, early-twenties blonde. Daniel would meet the Truebloods at breakfast in the morning.

Once he was safely ensconced in his room, he had phoned Mahina. He was shocked by her words..

"Tell me about it." He pulled out a chair from the room's desk and sat.

"The evil force—the one you knew about before you left?"

"Yes?"

"He has cast a hex on Tiare. It's a long story, but the end result is that the victim usually dies in three days."

"Three days!" Daniel stood, troubled.

"Yes, but you know Tiare. In her shaman way, she has the means to slow the process."

"Good . . . but . . . she's not able to heal herself?" He paced the room.

"Not yet, but she's working on it. It's a very black magic that even she does not fully understand."

"How is she doing?"

"As well as can be expected. She is still able to walk, but she has numbness to both of her legs, which she first noticed in her feet and is now up to her knees. If it reaches the level of her heart, she says, she will die."

Daniel blurted out, "I'm coming home."

Mahina said, "I appreciate your willingness to drop your investigation to come to our aid, but you cannot."

Daniel felt his face begin to burn, then shouted, "Why, not?"

"It might be best if I let Tiare explain—"

"Tiare? Isn't it three a.m. there?"

"It is. But, with her illness, I thought it best if she stayed at our home for now."

"I'm glad she is. But, Mahina, don't you think—"

Tiare was on the line. "Daniel?"

He regained his composure, sat down, cleared his throat and quietly spoke,"Yes. Mahina just shared the bad news with me. How are you doing?

"A little numbness in my legs, but otherwise I'm fine. You?"

"I'm in the middle of a rather puzzling set of murders, but I want come back to Rapa Nui."

"Why, Daniel?"

"It sounds like you need my help . . . don't you?"

Tiare sighed. "Daniel, certainly things are not going well, but I have dreamed about our situations, and my inner voice tells me that you need to stay right where you are."

"But—"

"Listen carefully, my friend. Assuming we all get through our trials, there will come a time in the not-too-distant future when you and Mahina will work together, hand-in-hand. But that moment is not now. You see, for the greatest growth, for the time being you must operate separately."

"But—"

"If *you* returned *here*, to Rapa Nui, Mahina would not be tested in the way necessary to be a strong shaman. And if *she* came to *your* assistance, you likewise would not develop the strength you need to be a great detective."

"But—"

"You both need to be tempered—hardened—like the blacksmith who heats metal red-hot to shape it properly. Daniel, you and Mahina are in the process of being formed and, if you came here, you would interrupt the development you both need. Do you understand?"

Tears welled in Daniel's eyes. "I do, but it doesn't feel very comfortable. In fact, I feel like someone is ripping my heart out."

Tiare explained, "True growth almost always goes hand in hand with pain. The greater the pain, the greater the growth. If everything was always easy, there wouldn't be a reason to be on this Earth."

"What if something bad happens? I couldn't bear it if anything harmful occurred to either of you, and I wasn't there to help."

Tiare sighed again. "Daniel, the future is not ours to worry about. All we can do is the best we can in the moment, and the outcome is not as important as our efforts. There's nothing I would like better than for the three of us to move through these difficult experiences unscathed. But there are no guarantees."

After a long pause, Daniel reluctantly understood the wisdom of her words. "Very well, then. I will stay here. Just in case I never speak to you again, I have words I wish to share with you."

"And what words are those?"

"Tiare, I love you. You have been my teacher and my guide, and I can never thank you enough. I *so* hope you find a way to stay in the world."

"Daniel, I love you too. Whatever the outcome, I believe the events taking place are happening for a reason. What that is, I don't yet know. But I am sure that someday we all will. Daniel, do you know any Sanskrit?"

"No, but isn't Sanskrit a language of India?"

"It is. In my learning on the Internet, I've enjoyed learning several different Sanskrit words. One of my favorites is Namaste."

Daniel asked, "Namaste? What does that mean?"

"Namaste means, 'The divine within me salutes the divine within you.' And so I say, Namaste, my friend."

Daniel was humbled. His voice was low and soft as he said, "Namaste, Tiare. I do hope the time comes when we can say it face-to-face."

"Let's plan on it. Do-na-da-`go-v-i."

Daniel smiled. Tiare had said goodbye to him in Cherokee. He repeated, "Do-na-da-`go-v-i."

Tiare chuckled, then said, "I thought you would enjoy hearing your native tongue. Now, before you go, Mahina wishes to speak with you again."

There was a brief silence.

"Dan-iel," Mahina said, with the voice he loved more than any other, "I want you to know that, under Tiare's guidance, I grow stronger every day. But no force of evil is greater than my love for you. I will see you again, I promise."

"I love you too. Please be careful."

"I will."

"Goodbye, Mahina."

"Goodbye, my love."

When he hung up the phone, Daniel held his head in his hands, tears flowing freely, shaken to his core.

If only I knew for certain that I would look upon her lovely face again.

But he didn't.

And there wasn't a damned thing he could do about it.

Chapter 15

Daniel tossed and turned in his bed; he couldn't stop worrying about Mahina and Tiare. His bedside clock read 3:15 a.m. Since he couldn't sleep, he flipped on the bedside lamp, sat up and pieced together the facts of the Stonehenge investigation, as he currently understood them.

First, even though Scotland Yard believed that the arrival of the non-Salisbury victims over a five year period was circumstantial, Daniel didn't think so. He found it incredibly suspect that some of the brightest minds in the world had been called to out-of-the-way Salisbury. *No doubt from a local core group.* He guessed their coming was spread out to avoid any suggestion they were connected. He was certain that it involved an extreme amount of wealth. *What else could uproot them from wherever they were?* The chef's unlikely move to Salisbury had cemented that thought in Daniel's mind.

He also knew that success for their endeavor did not come quickly, and gold had to be part of the equation. Daniel again wondered why the killer tried to hide that fact.

And who was the murderer? One of the group, one who desired more than his or her share of the wealth? Or was it an outsider who had somehow found out about the secret gathering and their clandestine plans and who was willing to kill as many as possible to obtain part of the fortune?

Yet, Daniel felt that the real key to solving this conundrum lay with the stolen bluestone. *How did it fit with the group's undertaking? Was the ensemble involved in some sort of research—a grand twenty year experiment?*

If so, the million-dollar question was: *What was that experiment?*

The dream he had on the plane also confounded him. It seemed clear that the amorphous mass that absorbed Mahina reflected his fears about what might happen to her.

But what about the phoenix?

Certainly, it represented a new beginning, life springing from death and a transformation of sorts, but what did that have to do with anything? Daniel trusted his subconscious mind to give him information in his dreams that was relevant. The problem was that most dreams were cloaked in metaphor and symbolism, and this one was no exception. It was up to him to figure out the meaning.

Besides all that, the acrid odor puzzled him. Before he went to bed that evening, he searched the Internet on his laptop. He could find no information that indicated the significance of that combination of odors.

He was missing something.

What is it?

Daniel's head swam. *Too many variables . . .* His mind jumped between his dream, the murders and back.

Daniel knew there was one constant theme in the murders: Greed—greed of the highest order. Daniel knew that anyone or anything that got in the way of obtaining this wealth would be eliminated.

He turned off the lamp and lay back in bed, uneasy. Tiare had told him the danger he would face would be at least as great as that which she and Mahina would confront. At last he understood her words.

Daniel finally drifted off into a light slumber.

His phone alarm woke him with the tune, "Question," by The Moody Blues. He usually preferred silence to music, but if there had to be one song to wake him up, it might as well be something that stirred his soul. When he heard it, how could the words not remind him of Mahina? His heart warmed at the thought.

Daniel would have liked to lie in bed and doze a bit more, but last night, when he was greeted by Lily, the employee of the bed and breakfast, he had made an appointment for breakfast at 8 a.m. When she had asked him if he had any dietary preferences, he told her he was a lacto-ovo vegetarian. Granted, he had not yet attained such a diet, but he hoped this would avoid the question of being served blood pudding, the thought of which made him shudder almost as much as when he ate the rats in ancient Rapa Nui.

After his shower, he dressed in his usual business attire, a black suit, black dress shirt without a tie, and black Merrell hiking shoes. Since he had finished his international travels for now, it was time to look more professional. As he prepared to walk out the door, he noticed a large white envelope had been slid under it. Written in blue ink on the outside was simply: *Hawk.*

Curious, he pulled the envelope out from under the door and sat down on his bed, covered with a hand-sewn quilt.

Daniel tore open the end of the envelope and pulled out a single piece of white paper, folded into thirds. He removed it and slowly opened it, being careful to touch only the edges. Centered in the middle of the page, were two names, handwritten in cursive:

Ian Johansen
Olga Alexeyeva

Daniel didn't recognize either name. He gingerly put the sheet back in the envelope and stuffed it in the inside pocket of his coat.

He locked the door to his room, walked down the wooden stairs and was greeted by the pleasant aroma of eggs and bacon. While he had sworn off eating bacon some time ago, the smell was still seductive.

The moment he walked into the breakfast area, he spotted a handsome couple who stood up from the table. The room had four maple-stained wooden dining tables, which were covered with elegant silverware, bright red napkins, sparkling white china and crystal glasses. No other patrons were in the room.

They both appeared to be in their seventies. The man was slender, had neatly combed white hair and wore a navy-colored sweater over a light blue shirt with a button-down collar. His slacks were black and loosely fitted.

"Why, Detective Fishinghawk!" the man exclaimed, "Gordon has told us all about you. We've known him since he was a little boy, so we just can't find it within ourselves to call him Inspector Green. He was such a bright lad; no wonder he's done so well as a detective. I understand you're called Hawk, is that right?"

"Yes."

He extended his hand and Daniel shook it. "Hawk, my name is James Trueblood, and this is my wife Emily."

"Hawk, so pleased to meet you," she said as she nodded her head. Quite the opposite of her husband, she was plump with dyed black hair, pinned up on top of her head. The buttons bulged outward on her dress, and it appeared as if she was barely able to squeeze into it. Her dress was white and sprinkled with large navy polka dots. It closely matched the color of her husband's sweater. She also wore a red apron embroidered with colorful chickens. Daniel wondered if they had dressed to coordinate with each other.

"Excuse me for a moment," she said, as a flying cockroach buzzed just past them, flitting from table to table in the dining room.

Daniel raised his eyebrows when Emily squealed with each and every landing. She grabbed a nearby flyswatter and crept up on it. With a deft snap of her wrist, the unwanted insect was crushed.

She quickly pulled a tissue from her apron pocket and picked up the dead bug. After throwing it into a nearby stainless steel rubbish bin, she took out what appeared to be a bottle of disinfectant from the pocket of her apron, and she sprayed and wiped, not only where the insect was crushed, but also in every place it had landed. The strong smell of rubbing alcohol confirmed his suspicion.

"For all we know," she muttered, "that beastly bug just came off a pile of bird crap. Don't worry. I'll have it clean in a jif."

"As you can see," James leaned over and whispered to Daniel, "my wife doesn't fanny around when it comes to germs. She—"

"Fanny around?" asked Daniel.

"Procrastinate. She's the cleanest person I know; she showers at least three times a day. And your bedding?"

"Yes?"

"Every bit of it, blankets and pillows, sheets and quilts, were laundered after the last clients. And you'll find no carpets in this home. All the floors are hard surfaced. They're easier to clean. Emily wouldn't have it any other way."

Daniel and James watched her as she feverishly moved on to cleaning light switches, door knobs and the seats of the chairs.

"I'm glad to see she's feeling better," James added. "There's a touch of a stomach bug going around the community, and she was up much of the night vomiting. Hawk, would you like to sit with me for a moment while she wipes up?"

"I'd love to."

"Lily saw you coming down the stairs and is preparing your breakfast. No blood pudding?" James asked, with a slight grin.

"I'm afraid not."

"Coffee or tea?"

"I prefer tea," Daniel replied. "Do you have Darjeeling?"

"Of course we do. We're British; we love all kinds of tea." James reached over into a small wooden box on the table, pulled out a square tea envelope and handed it to Daniel.

Daniel read the wrapping before he opened it: "An organic variety from the Risheehat Estate. Very nice." He removed the tea bag from the envelope, placed it in his cup and poured hot water on it from a red decanter resting on the table.

James sighed. "I'm afraid that's the last bag we have from Teas of the World, the shop owned by Penny Pumpernickel before she was killed."

"I'm sorry. Did anyone take over her store?"

A pained look on his face, James said, "Yes, a large tea company from London now runs it. It's not the same."

"I can only guess," Daniel said. "Large businesses can never replicate what sole proprietors do."

At that moment, Emily shrieked and sprinted across the room with flyswatter in hand, apparently pursuing a spider that made the poor decision of taking a stroll into the breakfast area.

James squinted, leaned forward and asked quietly, "Now, I understand you're here to investigate the murders we've been having."

"That's true. Have you heard anything that might be helpful?"

"Not a bit. Of course, gun violence in the UK is almost unheard of, so we're a bit bothered by all these happenings."

"I see. May I ask you some questions?"

"Of course," James answered.

"Is the front door of your bed and breakfast secured during the night?"

"No, it's left open for the convenience of any of our guests who might like to stay out late."

"Were you aware of anyone who might have come after I had gone to bed?"

"No, but I'll check with Lily. She was up later than we were."

"I'd appreciate that." Daniel patted the pocket of his coat and said, "I found an envelope under my door this morning with the names Ian Johansen and Olga Alexeyeva written on a sheet of paper inside it. Do these names mean anything to you?"

James said, "Why, yes, they do. They were immigrants to our city some years back—"

"How long ago?"

"That, I'm not sure of. If I had to guess, I'd say close to fifteen years."

Daniel caught his breath and tried not to show his surprise.

"Around two years ago, both went bloody insane, and since then they have been institutionalized at the local asylum. It's quite a shame. Those who knew them said they were both quite likeable and hard workers—" He lowered his voice and whispered, "Though rumor has it, the woman was a bit of a flirt and liked hanging around rough folks in bars."

"I see. Am I able to visit them?"

"I don't know why you couldn't. But why?"

"I've got the feeling that whoever left me this note knows something."

"Perhaps, but maybe he or she just wants to mislead you."

"Let's hope not," Daniel replied, "What's the name of the mental hospital?"

"It's the Healing Mind and Spirit Hospital, five kilometers east of town."

"Good, I'll call and see if I can pay them a visit."

"Capital idea."

Daniel was completely bewildered. If he had to guess, it seemed that two of the elite group had gone out of their minds.

Why?

Was it chance?

Daniel didn't think so.

Chapter 16

Mahina awoke early in the morning, thinking of Dan-iel. Darkness still covered all, and the sun had yet to bring light to the land of the Rapanui. She picked up the pillow from his side of the bed and held it to her face. She breathed deeply and still could appreciate his familiar, comforting scent.

How she longed to feel him lying beside her and feel the safety of his arms around her. She needed his strength right now, more than she could have ever imagined. Yet, she was aware that Dan-iel was also in danger, and she yearned to go help him. For now, though, as Tiare had said, it was time for them to do their work separately. But that didn't mean she wasn't worried about him.

She rose from the bed and dressed. Yesterday evening Tiare had promised to begin her next teaching session early in the morning, and Mahina wanted to be prepared. She walked into the living area and began to focus on her breath. It was hard to put aside her anxieties about Dan-iel, but she had to.

She had plenty of her own to deal with.

The sun was up, and Mahina was preparing a breakfast of waffles, poached eggs and orange juice, when she heard Tiare call her name from the second bedroom.

Mahina walked over to the closed door and knocked on it. "May I come in?"

"Please," Tiare weakly answered.

Mahina gasped and held her hand to her mouth when she entered and saw Tiare sitting on the edge of her bed, sweaty, pale and short of breath.

Tiare whispered, as if the simple act of speaking was difficult. "Mahina, things—things seem to have taken a turn for the worse. The numbness is now up to my waist, and I am having a difficult time walking. It was quite a struggle just to dress and get up to the bathroom."

"Oh, no."

"Yes, I'm afraid so. Please help me to the breakfast table. I'll try to eat some food, and then we must continue your lessons. If the hex continues at this rate, we will have little time to spare."

Mahina walked to Tiare, put her strong arms around her and guided her, step by step, into the dining area. She sat Tiare in a chair across from her at the table.

They began to eat, and after awhile Tiare said, "I have an idea I would like to share with you."

Seeing Mahina's nod, she went on. "Probably the most important thing to decide at this stage is what your work will be as a shaman. Like many shamans, it seems clear that you will be a dreamer, one who goes into deep meditation to gain insights that others normally would not have. To assist you on your spiritual journeys, you have already connected with your spirit animal, the red-tailed tropicbird, the *tavake*."

Mahina fondly remembered the sacred event.

"And since you are from the past, it would seem natural that you would be a keeper of the ways of the Rapanui, one who would carry on our ancient traditions."

"Certainly," Mahina concurred.

"Now, as I meditate deeply about you, I feel certain that you are also a healer."

Mahina looked astounded. "What makes you think that?"

"An energy surrounds you that feels restoring and comforting. As you know, my way of healing is with herbal preparations, but I don't believe that will be your approach. Have you ever heard of energy healing?"

Mahina felt confused "No, please tell me about it."

"All around us is a healing power, a life force that emanates from the sun, the air and the earth. Some call it *prana*, and some call it *chi*. Whatever, there are those who are naturally able to direct this energy into another person and help bring about balance and healing. I believe you are capable of this kind of work."

Mahina had a gleam in her eyes and urgency in her voice as she said, "Let's start now. May I practice on you?"

Tiare nodded her approval. "I would be honored. Have you finished with your breakfast?"

"I have," Mahina said as she took a last gulp of her juice.

"Good. For a moment, I want you to close your eyes, as I will. Let your mind concentrate on your in breath and out breath. We will do this together for a few minutes."

Student and teacher sat silently for a short time, then Tiare said, "Now, I want you to move your mind outside yourself, first expanding to the ceiling of this room, then above the house and up into the sky. Before too long, you will find yourself far above the Earth, looking down on our beautiful planet."

Mahina gasped with delight. "Yes! I see the continents, oceans and clouds. Where is our home island, Rapa Nui?"

"Our little isle is too small to see from the height where you are. I promise that someday, together, we will have a closer look from above."

"I would love that."

"Now," Tiare said, "this time, with your spiritual eye, look again at the world below and tell me what you see."

Mahina did not hesitate. "There is a white glow that extends beyond the Earth and into the sky. It is white, sparkling and shiny."

"Good, my student. What you are seeing is the energy field that emanates from our planet. Some call it an aura. Now, return to my side and look at me with your spiritual eye. What do you see?"

"Teacher, I see a similar light around you in the shape of a glowing egg."

"Excellent. What you are seeing is the aura around me. Now look in the middle of it and you will see a number of bright, spinning areas, called chakras, where the light is much brighter. Do you see them?"

"I do."

"How many do you see?" Tiare asked.

"Let me count them. Let's see . . . there are seven."

"Do you see any differences in them?

"Yes, they are all various colors, but there seems to be a problem. The one at the bottom is dull, not spinning and looks to be a pale shade of red. The next one up is barely orange, sluggish and not moving either. The one above that is yellow, a bit brighter and is spinning slowly. The chakra at the level of the heart is a sparkling green and spinning rapidly, much like the blue, indigo and violet ones above it."

"Very good, my student!" Tiare exclaimed. "Now, open your eyes. What you have just seen is the hex's effect on me. It brings about a blockage in my energy fields, my chakras. When it reaches the one at the level of the heart—the green one—and causes it to cease to spin, then I will die. Do you understand?"

Tears came into Mahina's eyes. "Yes . . . I do."

"Now, let's try a little experiment. Would you please help me over to the couch?"

"Gladly."

Mahina carefully assisted Tiare to the couch. She gently helped Tiare lie on her back.

"Mahina, pull up a chair and face the couch. Close your eyes and take a few deep breaths. Then hold your hands palms down and put them a few inches above my forehead. Tell me what you feel."

"Teacher, it feels warm."

"Good. Continue to move your hands down to just above my throat area and then over my heart."

"It still feels warm."

"Perfect. Now slide them to above my diaphragm and slowly move them to an area just above my pelvis."

A look of concern crossed Mahina's face. "From your diaphragm down it is cold—ice cold."

"Just as I thought," Tiare said. "Now, remember that sparkling light that you saw surrounding the Earth?"

"I do."

"I would like for you to pull that energy down from above you and bring it through the top of your head, down into your heart area. It's not as hard as you might guess. Let me know when you accomplish that."

Mahina concentrated deeply, and soon she felt a rush of a warm, pulsating light moving through her head and into the middle of her chest. She felt permeated with love.

"Now," she reverently whispered.

"Wonderful. Hold both of your hands palm down over my heart area and direct this glowing light from your heart down both of your arms and into my diaphragm. When you see the yellow chakra there begin to brighten and spin faster, move your hands down to just above my navel to the orange one. Again focus the light there, and, once it is revitalized, go down to the red chakra and repeat the process."

Tears rolled down Mahina's face as she felt the brilliant white light surge from the palms of both of her hands and into Tiare. After a period of intense concentration, Mahina could see that all of the lower three chakras had brightened and were now vibrant shades of yellow, orange and red. All were rapidly spinning.

Mahina rose up from Tiare, put her hands to her face and whispered a silent prayer of gratitude.

Tiare sat up straight and exclaimed, "Mahina—I can feel my legs again!"

As the two women embraced each other, Tiare said, "Thank you, my student. But, to be sure, would you survey me again with your hands?"

Mahina once again closed her eyes, breathed and checked the lower three chakras again. To her dismay, she noted the energy had improved but could tell that it was already beginning to fade.

Tiare slouched back on the couch and confirmed, "My student, I'm sorry to report that the numbness has returned. The healing was only temporary."

They sat in solemn silence for a few moments.

Finally, Tiare said, "We have learned two things today. First of all, it is clear that you have an innate ability to direct healing energy. Now we know this is to be part of your life's work.

"For me, though, the hex is too deep and powerful. I am convinced that you have the ability to slow this evil process but not cure it. This will buy us precious time for me to find some other way to deal with this. For that, I am most grateful."

Mahina appeared devastated. "But—"

Tiare interrupted and smiled, "No buts, my student, only acceptance. If I am meant to find an answer, I will, and I will search every possibility."

"Yes, teacher," she said, but fear had clutched her in its scaly, vise-like grip.

Mahina could not smile back.

Chapter 17

Daniel sat at the desk of head psychiatrist, Doctor Siegfried Kratz, of the Healing Mind and Spirit Hospital.

When Daniel had phoned the facility earlier, he was informed by the operator that, for him to visit a patient in the facility, he first had to get permission from Doctor Kratz. So, Daniel grabbed the only available appointment, knowing it would be difficult to make it there on time. He called Ned, quickly threw on some clothes, and dashed downstairs for a quick cup of tea.

Ned had come promptly, but said hardly a word the entire trip. He appeared to have on the same clothes he wore yesterday, though along with the odor of cheap wine, the stench of body odor found its way into the back of the car.

Daniel thought, *Getting an occasional bath is not high on Ned's list of things to do.*

Besides that, there was something troubling about Ned's demeanor. Daniel sensed he was hiding something—something dark and uncomfortable. He planned to discover what that was, as soon as possible.

After a short drive, Ned pulled onto the concrete driveway of the institution, which sat far back from the highway. The area was densely forested, and the road itself was lined with tall trees with branches that overhung the road, creating a canopy of barren limbs.

In the summertime, Daniel thought, *the area must be beautiful, but, in the dead of winter, it felt chilling and dreary.*

Once they'd arrived at the parking lot, Ned had insisted on waiting outside in the biting cold.

Daniel was about to enter the front door when he turned and saw Ned sitting in the car, smoking a cigarette and rubbing his hands together to keep warm.

Daniel had been ushered into Doctor Kratz's office by the receptionist, and he sat, waiting over thirty minutes for the doctor to arrive. As he looked at the hands of his watch as they swept past his appointment time, he wondered why, in general, doctors were such poor managers of time. Rarely was he was seen promptly when he went to see any physician, and Doctor Kratz was no exception.

Daniel was impressed by the office, which was painted a warm chocolate color. Behind the large, darkly stained wooden desk were not only Doctor Kratz's various diplomas, but also prominent and handsomely drawn illustrations of Sigmund Freud, Paracelsus and Hermann Rorschach, all looking quite serious and scholarly. Daniel sat in a maroon colored leather chair, with a crackling fireplace at his left, which gave the room a cozy, comfortable feeling.

A door opened to his right, and Doctor Kratz stiffly entered the room. He was of medium build, wore bronze wire-rimmed glasses and appeared to be in his mid-seventies. His gray hair was thinning, and a salt and pepper, neatly trimmed beard and moustache gave him a professional air. He wore a full-length, starched white medical jacket with "Siegfried Kratz, M.D.," embroidered in red script just above the jacket pocket, and coiled in the lower right pocket was a stethoscope.

"So you must be Hawk," said Doctor Kratz, in a barely noticeable Germanic accent. He looked at Daniel with tired green eyes and extended his hand in greeting.

Daniel shook it. "You're Doctor Kratz?"

"Yes," the doctor said, as he took his place behind the desk. He pulled a mahogany pipe out of the top drawer, held it in front of him and asked, "May I?"

"Certainly."

Doctor Kratz poured a measured amount of tobacco into the pipe chamber from a beige cloth bag lying on the desk. After tamping it down with his index finger and lighting it, he asked, "What can I help you with?"

"I need to interview two of your patients."

Kratz showed no emotion. "And why is that?"

"Police business. I'd rather not say why—for the time being."

Kratz exhaled a thick cloud of fragrant smoke in Daniel's direction. "Which patients?"

"Ian Johansen and Olga Alexeyeva."

Kratz stared at the floor. "You will not be able to speak with Ms. Alexeyeva."

"Why not?"

Kratz looked back up at Daniel. "She died just four days ago. Her cremated remains have already been shipped back to her family in Russia."

"What happened?" Daniel asked, but he thought, *How convenient.*

Kratz shrugged his shoulders. "She was wildly psychotic, and we were unable to control her with chemical restraints alone. In spite of maximal doses of many different drugs, she continued to be violent and dangerous, not only to herself but also to others. The staff had to keep her in a straitjacket twenty-four hours a day. Getting her to eat was nearly impossible, so we had to place a feeding tube through the wall of her abdomen and into the stomach.

"Mrs. Ambrose, the nurse who makes morning rounds, discovered her lying dead in her bed. Often, this sort of patient eventually dies from pneumonia because they are unable to move around and clear their secretions. Whatever, she died from natural causes."

"Was an autopsy done?"

With disdain, Kratz stated, "Of course not. There was no reason to do so. Her death was not expected, but it was predictable."

"Well, then, what about Mr. Johansen?"

"In many ways, he is like Ms. Alexeyeva—violent and uncommunicative—and he requires maximal restraint. I can't imagine you'd get any information out of him. And, like you Americans say, I believe you're barking up the wrong tree."

"I appreciate your concern, Doctor," Daniel said, his dark eyes flashing, "but I'd like to try anyway."

"What if I told you no?"

Daniel leaned forward in his chair and intensely stared at him. "Then tomorrow I'll be here with a subpoena, and I'll have my interview."

"As you wish, Hawk. I still think you're wasting your time, but if you insist, step outside my office and sit in the chair in the hallway. I'll page Mrs. Ambrose, who is also his nurse. She will take you to his room."

"A final question?" asked Daniel.

"If you must."

"Do you like wine?"

"Not at all. I haven't had a sip of wine since I was served a glass of *Auslese* as a teenager. I didn't like it then, and I'm sure my tastes haven't changed. Why?"

"Just curious," Daniel said as he walked out the door.

Mrs. Ambrose, in a white nursing uniform, approached Daniel after a short wait. She appeared to be in her late twenties and was petite and pale, with a scattering of freckles across the bridge of her nose. She had straight, bright-red hair pulled behind her head in a single braid, and a bruise was under her right eye, which had been partially concealed with makeup.

Daniel resisted the urge to ask her about the bruise.

"Sir, I understand you would like to speak with Mr. Johansen?"

"Yes, that is correct."

"You go by . . . Hawk?"

Daniel nodded. "Yes."

"I am Mrs. Ambrose. Follow me." She turned and walked down a dark hallway. The light blue linoleum floor and white walls were in stark contrast to the palpable warmth of Doctor Kratz's office. The place reeked of emptiness and Pine Sol, and felt cold in spite of the overheated hallway.

They approached a heavy, black-metal door, which Mrs. Ambrose opened by waving her employee badge in front of a sensor on the adjacent wall. It slowly creaked open.

"This is the ward where we keep our most dangerous patients."

They both walked through the entryway.

The doors heavy latch clicked shut behind them as they continued to walk, and Daniel felt cornered. His senses warned danger, and, yet he had to move onward. The walls seemed to be closing in on him and reminded him of being trapped in the painfully narrow passage in the time cave on Rapa Nui. He shuddered for a moment and but kept walking.

He soon heard the muffled sounds of insanity: screams, moans and rantings from behind the closed doors that they passed by.

"Frightening, isn't it?" Mrs. Ambrose said, flatly.

"Absolutely." He battled back his fears and asked, "Is this area under surveillance?"

She stopped and turned to face him under a flickering overhead light. "Night and day, every day."

"Do you mind if I ask you a few questions?"

Her timid brown eyes seemed to probe him. "Not at all."

"Good. On the night that Olga Alexeyeva died, were the cameras on?"

She looked at Daniel as if he were an idiot. "Of course they were. It wouldn't be safe otherwise."

"Are cameras in each room?"

"No, but the hallways are all monitored."

"Who watches the monitor?"

"A technician watches the screen as I tend to the patients."

Daniel bore down. "Who was watching it the night Alexeyeva died?"

"It was George. He did not report anything unusual."

Daniel put his fingers to his chin and nodded. "I see. When you found Alexeyeva, had she been dead for some time?"

"She was cold—so, yes."

Daniel tapped his foot impatiently. "What did you do next?" .

"I notified Doctor Kratz."

"Did he come to the room to check her?"

Ambrose voice raised slightly, and she tensely said, "He came immediately and examined her."

"No evidence of foul play?"

Her face burned red, which closely matched her hair. "Of *course* there wasn't. How *could* there be?"

"I apologize." Daniel spoke gently. "As an inspector, please appreciate that these are questions I have to ask."

"I understand," she replied, but now she had a look of distrust on her face. She resumed walking and finally stopped in front of a closed door, where, opposed to the other rooms, an eerie silence prevailed.

"Are you ready to see Mr. Johansen?"

Daniel tried to hide his anxiety. He nodded.

She opened the door with her badge. "I'll wait outside for you, just in case I need to grab some sedative medication. Remember, Mr. Johansen can be very violent. Don't say anything that might excite him."

Daniel's eyes widened, and he stopped before entering. "Isn't he restrained?"

"Yes, but that doesn't mean he can't find a way to escape. Keep your eyes on him at all times. Knock on the door when you are ready, and I'll get you out—immediately, if necessary."

Daniel grimaced at her words and walked into the beige rectangular room. He steeled himself as he heard the door click shut behind him. When Daniel looked back, he could see Mrs. Ambrose's face peering through a small wire-reinforced window in the door.

He turned back and faced the room.

On the opposite wall stood a bed on which Ian Johansen lay motionless, his upper body wrapped in a white, high-collared straitjacket and his black-socked feet tied by straps to the rails at the foot of the bed. At the side was a bed stand, with a square basin setting on top, a blood-stained rag hanging on its side.

Daniel quietly stepped over to a folding chair by the bedside and sat.

Ian Johansen was a very tall man, well over six feet, and he appeared emaciated. Daniel guessed that, in his prime, Johansen was muscular and took long strides.

But not now.

Daniel took a closer look. Mr. Johansen had long, straight tangled blonde hair that looked like it hadn't been washed in some time. He had a fine, dark beard and moustache, and he appeared to be sleeping. A yellow discharge pooled in the inside corners of his eyes and dried drops of pus were crusted on his cheeks

"Mr. Johansen? Mr. Johansen?"

No response.

Daniel spoke louder and gently touched his shoulder. "Mr. Johansen?"

Slowly, Johansen's bloodshot eyes opened and stared at Daniel with a look of pure hate. To Daniel, the energy emanating from him felt like that of a feral animal.

"Mr. Johansen, I'm Detective Daniel Fishinghawk. Can you talk to me?"

Johansen's face turned purple and he gritted and ground his rotten, black teeth. Daniel heard the distinct snap of a tooth breaking and blood oozed from the corner of Johansen's mouth. He thrashed from side to side as he yelled out, "*Nooooo . . . Nooooo . . .*"

"What do you mean?"

"It's gone bad—it's all gone bad!" Johansen sputtered out.

Daniel jerked to the side as Johansen coughed, barely dodging a wad of dark green sputum.

"The phoenix . . ."

"Phoenix?" Daniel questioned, astonished.

"Don't you know?" He hissed as he spoke.

"No, I don't. Tell me."

"I can't tell anyone or I will die."

"You won't die," Daniel reassured him.

"*Gold!*" Johansen was wild-eyed as he screamed even louder. "*Gold!*"

"What about gold?"

"*Nooooo* . . . I can't say! If I tell you, you will die too."

A shiver went up Daniel's spine. He reassured himself more than Ian Johansen when he said, "I won't die."

Suddenly, the leg restraints ripped apart and the skeletal man somehow tore the straitjacket from his chest.

Daniel leaped from his chair, but before he could move away, Johansen stood over him, his surprisingly strong hands grasping the lapels of Daniel's coat. He grinned an evil grin, and a fetid odor exuded from his mouth. Daniel could hear the door behind him beginning to open.

Hurry, Daniel thought. *Oh, God, hurry!*

Johansen growled, "Oh, yes you will."

Daniel pulled Johansen's hands from his coat and forced him back onto the bed. Johansen fought with superhuman strength—like a man possessed.

At that moment Mrs. Ambrose quickly stepped in and injected her patient's thigh with a full syringe of yellow fluid. A few struggling moments later, Johansen went limp. Mrs. Ambrose went back into the hallway then reappeared with new leg restraints and straitjacket. She reapplied them, and once she was certain they were secure, she and Daniel returned to the hallway. She pulled the door securely shut behind them.

"That's the fourth set of leg restraints and straitjackets this week," she whispered to Daniel.

Daniel was incredulous. "Why didn't you tell me?"

"I did, in a way," she said with a wry smile. "Sometimes it's good to find these things out by yourself."

"Thanks for nothing," Daniel said, irritated.

Daniel perspired heavily as he followed Mrs. Ambrose back down the hallway.

Why did Johansen mention the phoenix?

Why did he talk about gold?

What in the hell is going on around here?

Daniel abruptly stopped. He had to see something else.

"Mrs. Ambrose? I want to visit Olga Alexeyeva's room."

"Why? It's empty," she replied, with a hint of annoyance in her voice.

"It's part of my job."

She sighed, her anger seeming to fade to acceptance. "I suppose it wouldn't hurt anything. Here, it's the next room on your right. Let me open the door for you."

She again used her badge to open the door. She stepped aside as Daniel entered.

He slowly walked through the door, trying to put aside what had just happened so he could focus his attention entirely on the room. It was a mirror image of Johansen's, only the bed was unoccupied and made up with crisp white linens, a gray blanket overlying it. Daniel scanned the room, looking over every inch, inhaling deeply. The odor of Pine Sol was especially strong in the room and drowned out all other smells. *Probably*, he reasoned, *because it had been freshly cleaned.*

But then again, could it be? Was there was another scent in the background?

He carefully walked to the head of the bed and sat in another institutional folding chair. He closed his eyes, inhaling even more deeply. To his surprise, there was another subtle odor. He put aside the overpowering smell of Pine Sol and focused entirely on the background scent. It was faint, very faint.

Am I imagining things?

Surely not—yet—there it was—maybe?

Chanel Number Five?

Daniel's head spun with confusion, and he couldn't leave the Healing Mind and

Spirit Hospital quickly enough. Not pausing to say farewell to Doctor Kratz, he strode through the front doorway and stepped outside into the penetrating cold.

As he approached the car, he caught his breath.

One neatly placed bullet hole was in the windshield, and Ned sat in the front seat, a gaping wound in his forehead. Blood covered his face. His mouth was open, and his dried tongue hung off to the side.

His eyes stared straight ahead—at nothing.

He was dead.

Chapter 18

Mahina and Tiare sat on 'Anakena beach, watching and listening to the sea birds that flew overhead. The sounds were mesmerizing, and soon both teacher and student closed their eyes, absorbing the atmosphere of peace.

Closely watching over them was the Ahu Ature Huki, the ancient *moai* Daniel had once sat before in meditation to find his way back to the present from the past. And, of course, this was where Daniel and Mahina chose to get married. A benevolent energy surrounded the two women, and any danger that might have presented itself seemed far away.

Tiare said, "Perhaps, Mahina, you are wondering why I have asked you to drive us to this place."

"I believe I know, but please tell me your thoughts."

"Very well. Part of shamanistic practice is to connect with your ancestral spirits. As I'm sure you realize, just because your loved ones are in spirit, it doesn't mean that the relationship and love you shared goes away. The link you established with your ancestors, while living, will always be there, and it is especially powerful in this location—where you previously lived."

Mahina nodded.

"Just think of all the *moai* our predecessors have carved. They represent the blessings and the *mana*—the power—of our ancestors, always protecting and guiding us.

"So it is natural for you to connect with your loved ones who have passed on before. Besides, one of your duties as a shaman will be to assist others to travel into the world of spirit, the Otherworld, so that they might visit their deceased family. It will be your sacred responsibility to provide such a service. So, for this, you must take your own journey. I cannot go with you—"

"Why not?" Mahina felt much safer in the land of spirit, knowing Tiare was at her side.

"Precious student, as you are aware, a time will come when I will not be around. When that will be, I do not know, but you must become accustomed to venturing into the Otherworld without me."

Seeing Mahina's disappointed look, she added, "I suggest, in the beginning at least, that you connect with your spirit animal, which will no doubt be willing to guide you through the realms of spirit. The one concern I have is that the one who wishes us harm resides in the Land of the Dead—"

"Land of the Dead?"

"Yes. This is a gloomy region of spirit where confused souls live, perhaps not realizing they are dead, still attached to their earthly life. At some point, though, they will eventually find their way to the other side.

"In our case, this wicked entity walks the Land of the Dead, hoping for the moment when he can harm us. His hate drives him, and that is why he has ventured into the darkest of the dark places to learn how to cast the Death Prayer."

"Can you tell me who he is?"

"When I am certain, I will. As I have said, he has been quite successful in cloaking his identity. But for now, I am sure that your spirit guide, the *tavake*, will know how to avoid the Land of the Dead and will safely lead you to your destination and back. Are you ready?"

"I am."

"Good. Now, before you begin, you should know that there are three levels where you can enter into the world of spirit: The lower, the middle and the upper. As time allows, I will instruct you on how to penetrate all three. But, for now, the best place to visit your ancestors is to go into the upper world. Traditionally, this could be accomplished by concentrating on smoke that is rising into the sky, a rainbow, a sunbeam, a tree or, at night, a star in the sky. What you are trying to do is find a thin place—"

"Thin place?"

"Yes, thin place, where the boundary between the earthly and spiritual worlds is paper-thin, and passage between the two planes of existence is much easier than at other locations."

Mahina nodded her understanding.

"Here, on Rapa Nui, one of my favorite ways to enter the upper world exists at the base of a *moai*. I follow the pathway, which seems like a tunnel, upward, through the *moai*, until I emerge into the spiritual worlds.

"For you, when you enter the Otherworld in this way, call upon your spirit animal to join you and let her know the reason for your journey. From that point, she will guide you in the proper direction. Please remember one thing: Shamanic journeys are a mixture of the expected and unexpected. They never happen the way you think they should. So be prepared."

Mahina steadfastly said, "I will."

Tiare hugged her. "Happy journeys, sister. At the onset, I will rhythmically click two rocks together. No matter how far you have ventured in your spiritual travel, a small part of you will be able to hear this. After awhile, when I sense your journey is close to ending, I will tap the rocks together more rapidly. This will alert you that the time of your quest approaches its end.

"Of one thing, I am certain: You likely will not want to come back. Celtic mystics have called the Otherworld a land of youth, beauty, health, abundance and joy, so it is certainly understandable that you would want to linger, perhaps longer than you should."

With a knowing look in her eyes, Tiare added, "Trust me, I know."

"Now, another serious matter. If you hear the rocks tapping even faster, you must *urgently* return. I will not be with you, so this is a signal that I am sensing danger, and you must come back as swiftly as possible. Now, Mahina, close your eyes and breathe."

The rhythmic sound of the clicking began, and Mahina directed her consciousness to focus intently on the tapping. Simultaneously, she timed her breathing with it.

In breath—*tap—tap—tap*

Out breath—*tap—tap—tap*

In breath—*tap—tap—tap*

Out breath—*tap—tap—tap*

After some moments had passed, she slowed her breathing even more, increasing the number of taps heard between each breath. When Mahina could barely hear the tapping, she directed her consciousness to the base of the *moai* at Ahu Ature Huki.

To her surprise, as Tiare had said, there was an etheric tunnel in the middle of the *moai*, and Mahina followed the channel up, accelerating until her spiritual body exploded out of the top.

When Mahina emerged, she stood in what could best be characterized as a land of pastels. The colors were paradoxically more brilliant, yet at the same time softer and easier on the eyes. The best way she could describe it was when Dan-iel had shown her the movie, *The Wizard of Oz*. The Earth she lived in seemed like shades of black and white as compared to the Otherworld.

Mahina was entranced by the lushness of the foliage, and she delighted in the aroma of sweetly fragrant bushes, much like wisteria, which wafted in the air around her. Somewhere in the far distance, Mahina could appreciate a slow, rhythmic clicking together of rocks.

Tiare . . .

Reminded of the task at hand, she closed her eyes and whispered a silent prayer. In moments, she heard distinctive guttural squawks, followed by high-pitched, whistle-like screeches and the flapping of wings. Suddenly, perched on the branch of a tree beside her, was a beautiful white bird with a long plume of red tail feathers.

The *tavake*.

The bird leaped from the branch and hovered in front of Mahina.

Come with me.

Mahina followed the flitting, magnificent bird along a grassy pathway as it cavorted through the brilliant blue sky. The temperature of the air was neither hot nor cold, and a light breezed danced through her hair as she strolled along. The path Mahina was on began a gradual incline, yet she did not feel fatigued.

The *tavake* led her up a heavily forested slope, and when Mahina turned a corner of the trail, a clearing emerged. It led to a high cliff overlooking a calm, blue sea. She sat cross-legged in the grass and studied the peaceful ocean. The *tavake* fluttered down beside her and looked at her quizzically.

Mahina turned to the bird and thought, *I wish to be guided to my ancestors. Who?*

Mahina thought about her father and mother.

Very well, they will be here soon. I shall return when it is time for you to go.

As the bird disappeared, Hotu Iti and Tavake, her parents, materialized before her. Mahina was pleased that they looked much younger than they did when she saw them in her earlier vision. They beamed at her as they both leaned forward to hold her in a lengthy embrace. Her father was stout and wore a white feather headdress, carefully placed upon his head. From his neck hung wooden ornaments, no longer stained with blood. Her mother was shapely and attractive, with her thick, brown hair tumbling well below her shoulders and onto her bare chest.

Mahina's eyes misted and she was barely able to say, "I've missed both of you . . . so, so much. It seems like just the other day . . . we were together. How are my brothers, Kai and Poki?"

Hotu Iti answered and his deep, resonant voice. "They are fine, and you would have been proud of the strong young men they became. And yes, while to you it must seem like just yesterday, we lived many more years before our lives peaceably ended."

Her mother, Tavake, added, "We are aware that you have been concerned about your absence from our lives, that it created hardship for us. We missed you terribly, yet we were both very happy to give you up to spend the rest of your life with your love, Dan-iel."

"You didn't die at the hands of warriors?" Mahina asked.

"No, daughter," Hotu Iti confirmed.

Mahina took a deep breath. "Father and mother, you both must know my time here is short. What would you have me know?"

Hotu Iti spoke. "First of all, we are both proud of the strong woman you have become."

Her mother, nodded in agreement.

"We also are aware of your decision to be a shaman, and we feel great happiness with your choice. But we also suspect this puts you at enormous risk. As I believe you already realize, an evil force wishes you harm. Very soon you will confront him, sooner, perhaps, than you might guess. Keep your guard up at all times, not only for you and Dan-iel, but also for your people, who need you very much."

The *tavake* bird reappeared, and from the distance Mahina heard an increased frequency of the tapping of the rocks.

"I must go," Mahina sadly told them. Tiare was right. She did not want to leave.

"We understand," her mother said. "When you have completed your shaman training, you can visit as often as you would like, but living your earthly life, with its joy *and* pain, is far more important."

"What you say is true, but you'll always be dear to me, and I will see you again," Mahina said as they all stood and once again embraced. "Farewell, my loved ones. Give my best to Kai and Poki."

"And you to Dan-iel," both said, just before they disappeared.

The *tavake* once again darted down the path, Mahina following close behind.

As they approached the portal, an aged woman approached, tottering on a gnarled cane. She wore a black robe and cape, with a hood that covered most of her pale face.

She stumbled up to Mahina. "Would you help an old woman? Take my hand."

Mahina reached up out to grasp it, the *tavake* issued a loud screech. The bird flew between Mahina and the woman, hanging in the air, again screeching a loud warning.

Mahina heard the *tavake*'s voice shouting in her head: *Stay away from her—do not take her hand. Quickly—to the moai!*

Rocks, far in the distance, clicked frantically.

Mahina sprinted to the moai as fast as she could run. Just before she entered the portal, she glanced back.

The old woman was no more. Standing in In her place stood a tall man in his late forties, with long, straight, black hair, streaked with white and tied behind his head. A deep scar marred his right forehead, extending into his scalp. He wore the same dark robe as the aged woman, only now the hood was retracted. The man laughed hysterically then, with a *poof*, disappeared.

Mahina shuddered at what she had just seen: The evil shaman of the ancient Rapanui, the one responsible for the cannibalism and murder of many innocent people. A person she feared more that anyone in the Universe.

Paoa.

Chapter 19

The evening of Ned's murder, the three detectives, Gordon Green, Edward DeWoody and Daniel Fishinghawk, sat in a conference room at the Bourne Hill Police Station, located in the central part of Salisbury. The walls were a dreary olive color, and a dim light overhung the square, burnished metal table at which they sat. On the wall facing Daniel hung a poster that exclaimed, in bold, black letters, "Don't Drink & Drive!" A faint odor of moth balls drifted through the air.

Earlier that day, after Daniel had discovered Ned's body, Green was summoned, posthaste, back to Salisbury, and the meeting had been set up after his arrival.

Daniel asked Green, "How's the Queen?"

"Still alive and kicking. Seems the plot on her life was a hoax. We've caught the daft idiot who set it all up, and I'm guessing he'll be in custody for a bit. Now, let's get on with it. DeWoody, what do we know so far?"

"The autopsy on Ned—which we put a rush on—except for the single gunshot wound to the head, showed nothing exceptional. Of course, it will take some time before the toxicology and microscopic examinations are completed. The pathologist, though, discovered something unexpected. A crude homemade tattoo was found on his chest, a heart with an arrow through it, with the initials N and L in the middle. Looked like it had been there for awhile."

"Blimey!" Green exclaimed, "Did you—"

"No need to ask, inspector. As you may know, Ned's parents were killed some years ago in a car crash, and he had no brothers or sisters. So, the Yard has been at it all day, chatting up teachers, old mates—anyone they could turn up from his past. I'm sorry to say there were no young ladies whose first name began with an L. Oh, there was a Grace, a Chloe, an Abigail—and so on—but no Layla, no Lucy, no Lola. I'm afraid the tattoo, for now at least, is a dead end."

"Not that it would have helped," said Green, dejectedly.

"Agreed. We also thoroughly searched Ned's home. What a rattrap! A one-room flat stacked to the ceiling with dishes overflowing with rotten food crawling with maggots. The place was entirely infested with roaches, rats, mice and anything else that crawls or flies. The odor was worse than anything I've ever experienced, and I thought for awhile we would need to engage an exterminator before we could inspect it. Finally, though, we were able to fight off the vermin and had a view of the place. Other than being the worst living quarters I have ever seen, we could find nothing that might lead us to his killer."

"That's too bad," Daniel said, still distracted by the initials.

DeWoody added, "Now, we've already checked the ballistics on the bullet that killed him, and it's the same weapon—a Glock pistol—that was used at Stonehenge and in all of the other murders. Unfortunately, no one saw or heard Ned's killing. It's my guess a silencer was used."

"Any recordings of the shooting?" asked Green.

"The only surveillance cameras are *inside* the hospital," DeWoody answered, with a shrug. "No one is worried about who drives up, but what their patients are doing is an entirely different matter."

Green nodded at DeWoody. "Congratulations, inspector, you've put in quite a day's work."

DeWoody blushed slightly. "Thank you, sir."

Green turned to Daniel. "Hawk, you were there when Ned's murder occurred. What did you turn up?"

"Not much. As you know, I was there to check on the two names on from the list I found slid under my door. One passed away four days ago, though her death 'was not unexpected,' according to staff. I did inspect the room where she died, and I thought—and I'm not sure about it—I detected the faint hint of a distinctive perfume."

"Really? Which one?"

"Chanel Number Five."

Green said, "I don't know that scent."

Daniel said, "Oh, yes you do. Chanel Number Five was the fragrance worn by Madame Girard the day we visited her house."

Green and DeWoody looked astonished.

"I know what you're wondering," Daniel added. "I've already checked, and she has an iron-clad alibi."

"And that is?" DeWoody expectantly leaned toward Daniel.

"Olga Alexeyeva died the night before Madame Girard's husband was killed. As Green already knew, she was with her husband that evening at the restaurant. The cameras at her home show her entering the home later and leaving the next morning, exactly the time period when Alexeyeva died."

"Well, it was a worthwhile thing to check out," Green commented. "Did the doctor inspect her after she died?"

"He did, and he said she died from natural causes."

"Well, then, we're done with that one," Green said. "Were you able to speak with the other gentleman that was on the list?"

"His name was Ian Johansen, and yes, I did."

"And?"

"All gibberish, it seemed. He mentioned something about gold; but, otherwise, I couldn't make any sense of anything he said." Daniel thought better about saying anything about the phoenix.

DeWoody said, "Well, he is in the nut house for a reason."

"True," Daniel agreed. "But don't you think it's a bit strange that two people, both who arrived from out of country around the same time, lost their minds close to two years ago?"

"Sorry, Hawk, I don't get the connection," Green said. "I know you believe that this whole thing is a conspiracy that was cooked up around fifteen to twenty years ago, but I still think it's a bloody coincidence. It's just too big of a leap of faith."

DeWoody nodded concurrence.

Daniel held his tongue and said no more.

"Anything else?" asked Green of the two.

DeWoody spoke first. "Yes. We've lifted the fingerprints from the paper that Hawk discovered under his door, and they are definitely Ned's. Besides, the handwriting matches. We've interviewed Lily, the helper at the Salisbury Bed and Breakfast, and, after seeing a picture of him, she's fairly certain she caught a glimpse of Ned as he exited the bed and breakfast that night."

Daniel said, "Inspector Green, you've grown up in this town. What do you know about Ned?"

"I know a bit more than the average person. Before we hired him as your driver, we ran a thorough background check. Ned was a chemical engineer who worked in Salisbury at a branch of a pharmaceutical company headquartered in London. Ned was a specialist in new drug development."

"Chemical engineer?" Daniel asked, surprised. "He must have been very bright."

"Yes," Green said, "believe it or not, he got his degree at Cambridge."

"What?" exclaimed Daniel, recalling Ned's filthy appearance.

"Oh, yes," Green said. "He was quite brilliant, and I've been told he was altogether a dapper young man in those days, but, about three years ago, he quit his job with the company, and since that time his life had spiraled downward."

"What do you think happened?" Daniel asked.

"No one seems to know. He lost his home and basically survived by having a taxi service. I wanted to give him a helping hand by hiring him to drive you around, but I was about to fire him, as I was reasonably sure he had a drinking problem."

No doubt about that, thought Daniel

Daniel was ready to speak his mind. "Gentlemen, I think we have to assume that Ned was killed because of the information he gave us. Ned believed that those names were important to our investigation, and, for some reason—God knows why—he decided to leak them to *me*. Clearly, the killer eliminated him before there could be any further disclosures. Can we agree on that?"

Both Green and DeWoody nodded.

"So, if we know why those names were important, then we'll at least have part of the answer to this mystery. Do either of you have any ideas?"

Neither man offered more.

"Think about it," Daniel added. "This is a classic case of not seeing the forest for the trees. The key questions are: Why was a bluestone taken from Stonehenge? Why was the obtaining of it so critical to the killer? When we know that, I believe that everything else will fall into place. What do you think?"

DeWoody shrugged his shoulders.

Green said, "I have no idea. Hawk, what do you suggest we do next?"

Daniel said, "To get the understanding I need, I'll have to investigate further the mystery of the bluestone. Where did you say it came from?"

"The Preseli Hills—in Wales."

"How long would it take to get there?"

"By train, about five and a half hours."

"Since you're the head of the investigation, may I have your permission to take a trip there?"

"Hawk, I can't imagine how rummaging around in a pile of rocks will be of any benefit whatsoever. But I know you are not a conventional detective. You proved that on Easter Island. I may not understand your methods, but I'll be happy to give you leeway in this situation. When do you want to leave?"

"Tomorrow morning."

"Good. I will call the Yard and ask my secretary to make the rail and hotel arrangements. She will call you back later tonight and give you the details."

Daniel added. "I know the doctor said the death of Olga Alexeyeva was due to natural causes, but I'm not convinced. The entire hospital scenario doesn't seem right to me. So, when I'm gone, Inspector DeWoody, would you please check the surveillance camera recordings taken at the Healing Mind and Spirit Hospital on the night that Alexeyeva died?"

"I'll be happy to."

Green glanced at his fellow detectives. "Are we finished?"

"I believe so." Daniel pushed back from the table.

DeWoody nodded in affirmation.

They all stood up and worked their way outside, through the bustling police station and into the bitter-cold, late evening air.

"Hawk, I'll give you a lift back to your bed and breakfast," Green said.

"Thanks."

Daniel stopped just before he entered the car; he felt a pair of eyes staring intently at him. Following his intuition, he looked up into a nearby tree and saw a large hawk with a dark brown head and wings, horizontally oriented brown and white stripes on its chest and neck.

Daniel searched his photographic memory. It was a Eurasian sparrowhawk, locally known as a sparrowhawk. Daniel felt wisdom in the gaze of the bird and started to walk toward it when the bird took flight and disappeared into the evening sky.

"Hawk, is everything okay?" Green asked, noticing his delay.

"Everything is fine," Daniel said as he entered the car, thinking of the intensity of the bird's stare.

Daniel and Green both missed another pair of eyes that watched their every step.

Ones that did not wish them well.

Chapter 20

"Paoa." Tiare said quietly. "I had suspected him, but now the identity of our stalker is certain."

Mahina was still trembling. The comfort of the warm beach, the bright sunshine and even Tiare's company, offered little solace. She asked, "I thought you said he only walked the Land of the Dead?"

"True, but I might guess he has used his dark magic to project an image of himself into the Otherworld. Even if you had taken his hand, I don't believe you would have been harmed. But, then again, Paoa is a master of the workings of the spiritual planes, and normal rules don't seem to apply to him."

Mahina rubbed the goose bumps on her arms. "What do we do next?"

Tiare had a pained look on her face. "I have no choice but to try once again to enter the dark place where Paoa obtained his magic. There, I have a chance to find a solution to the Death Prayer. To my knowledge, no one has ever been able to cast such a hex after they were dead. Paoa has information I do not, and, until I discover that, I have no way to correct this ailment."

Tiare saw Mahina's eyes mist with tears. "Certainly, the healing treatments you have been giving me have slowed the progress of the Death Prayer, but it is advancing and will soon reach my heart, which means certain death."

Mahina wiped her eyes. "We will find an answer before then."

"I certainly hope so. For now, you must continue to do your work to become a shaman. If I am overcome by the Death Prayer, you must be prepared to stand up to Paoa on your own."

"I am frightened to think of facing him by myself."

Tiare had a grim look on her face. "I understand, sister, I understand."

Mahina asked, "Should I ask Dan-iel to return? Could he help?"

"He would never arrive here in time. Everything will be taking take place in the next few days, not weeks. Daniel is the most brilliant man I have ever met, but I doubt he could do anything about our predicament. Daniel is, in many ways, like a shaman, but you are far more advanced in your training than he. He would be no help in your battle against a spirit entity, but especially one that is a shaman. You are far better equipped to deal with such a challenge.

"Besides, I am certain that he is facing an evil at least as great as the one we are confronting. He must deal with that before he leaves for home, for, if he does not, the evil will grow and spread, much like a cancer. It must be snuffed out now."

"I see," Mahina said, disheartened and afraid.

Tiare said, "Now, let us be off to your home. There, I need to do some very deep spiritual work. If an answer is obtainable, I must discover it. And you also must get in touch with your inner strength, and, even more importantly, you must rest. The time is rapidly approaching when we will have a face-to-face conflict with Paoa. I am certain he will have all sorts of tricks up his sleeve to use against us. We must be prepared."

"And we will be," Mahina affirmed, as confidently as she could.

How I wish I could be certain.

Chapter 21

Daniel sat in the train to Wales and watched the scenery from his window. He enjoyed seeing the well-manicured English countryside and going through small towns that were laden with British flavor. He grinned as he observed old couples taking their morning walks with dogs following behind them. Quaint row houses, each with individual chimneys, stood side by side, much like soldiers at attention.

The train was quiet, clean and comfortable. Daniel's first and only change of trains would occur in Cardiff, the capitol of Wales. From there, he would travel to Haverfordwest, where he would pick up his rental car—previously reserved by Green's secretary—and venture into the Preseli Hills. No maps were necessary; he had carefully scanned several before he left Salisbury and the images were forever imprinted in his memory.

Daniel continued to be concerned about Mahina and Tiare. He had tried to phone them before he left Salisbury, but got no answer, and, unfortunately, the cell service with his new UK SIM card was nonexistent in the rural areas. He would have to wait to call again until he arrived at his lodging later that evening.

Daniel remembered what the Dalai Lama had once said about worrying: "If a problem is fixable, if a situation is such that you can do something about it, then there is no need to worry. If it's not fixable, then there is no help in worrying. There is no benefit in worrying whatsoever."

Daniel shrugged his shoulders and grimaced. *Easy for him to say.*

Intuitively, Daniel knew the situation for Mahina and Tiare was approaching critical. In spite of the danger to them and the talk about the Death Prayer, he felt confident that the two of them could manage just about anything—Death Prayer or no Death Prayer. As he mentally debated again the idea of returning to Rapa Nui to be with them, he also was reminded of his responsibilities in England and the reasons he had come.

As he thought of Tiare's previous arguments, he once again realized he needed to stay, so instead of worrying, Daniel directed warm and healing thoughts to Mahina and Tiare. As the train hypnotically moved along the tracks, he slumbered and fell into a dream.

>Daniel found himself in the time cave, headed to ancient Rapa Nui.
>*Hadn't Salvador Diaz had it dynamited?*
>*Guess not*, he answered himself.
>He held a flashlight and easily picked his way along the damp floor. Shortly, he came to the narrow portion again, but he was not concerned. He had made it through twice, and he was sure the third time would not be a problem. In spite of the close quarters, Daniel maneuvered through the cave and walked toward a distant dot of light, one that he knew was the entrance to the past.
>Arriving at the portal, Daniel squeezed through the opening and strolled along the familiar trail until he came to the village of 'Anakena. He walked toward the hut of Hotu Iti and Tavake and was pleased to see them both standing out front.
>"Dan-iel!" Hotu Iti exclaimed. "What a pleasant surprise."
>"Where is Mahina?" Tavake asked.
>"She is still in the future."
>Hotu Iti's demeanor grew somber. "I see. Then that must be where Paoa is."
>"Paoa? He's dead."
>"No, he's not," Tavake told Daniel. "He was just here a short time ago. He said he was going to see Mahina."
>"Mahina?" Daniel was startled. "I'm sorry . . . I . . . I must be going.

Goodbye!"

He dashed back to the time cave. The moment he entered, he heard a loud explosion—like dynamite—and dust and debris shot out of the cave. The entryway collapsed.

No! he thought. *How do I get back?*

Daniel heard a loud roar of wicked laughter in his mind. A laugh he was all too familiar with.

Paoa.

Daniel awoke in a cold sweat, the train still rumbling down the tracks. As he wiped his forehead with his handkerchief, he silently questioned himself: How is this possible? Paoa is dead... isn't he?

Then Daniel realized—much to his dismay—that the spirit of Paoa could never die.

As Daniel focused his mind, he realized that Paoa was now an *akuaku*, a ghost who roamed the island of Rapa Nui, one who hated him, Mahina and Tiare with every fiber of his being. A wicked one who had somehow learned to cast the Death Prayer from beyond the grave.

And here I am, a world away.

Mahina, my dearest, be strong.

Chapter 22

Tiare tossed and turned in her sleep, restless. She glanced at her bedside clock—4:20 a.m.

Over the past few days, she had spent most of her time in deep meditation. She tried repeatedly to penetrate the dark areas, where Paoa had learned his secrets, but she had no success. She intuited that she had been barred from entering and, knowing Paoa, it was likely that he had used black magic to stop her from exploring black magic. She grimaced at the odd paradox, as she recognized her dire circumstances in it.

Tiare had run out of answers, though, and this disturbed her greatly. She had always believed any and every problem had a solution, one that could be found if one looked hard enough.

Not this time.

Further, her physical health was declining rapidly. The numbness was now close to the level of her heart, and her difficulty in walking grew even worse. She doubted she could move from her bed without assistance.

As Tiare looked inside herself with her spiritual eye, she could see that the yellow chakra at the level of the diaphragm was now dull and immobile. Even worse, the green chakra at the level of her heart had faded appreciably and was barely moving. When it stopped, she would die,-and she expected that to happen sometime within the next twenty-four hours.

Of course, Mahina's treatment in the morning would temporarily revitalize her, but, even with that, there was no stopping the inexorable decline, and she was certain today would be the day of reckoning: the day Paoa would confront them.

Without doubt, the ultimate target for Paoa's revenge was not her, but Mahina, the one who had previously killed him by throwing a spear through his head, thwarting his moment of great triumph. By her act, Mahina had prevented a bloody, violent takeover of Rapa Nui.

Tiare did not know Paoa as well as Mahina did, yet her intuition told her he would not wait for Tiare to die to spring his attack. His ego was so large and his hatred so great, he would have Tiare witness his assault on her apprentice. He desired to watch Tiare squirm helplessly as she heard Mahina scream in tortured misery.

Tiare was certain, though, that Paoa had badly underestimated Mahina's ability as a shaman, and this one fact gave Tiare a small measure of hope. Considering her early stage of training, Mahina was a very strong shaman, one of the most capable Tiare had ever known. And, when she finished her apprenticeship, Tiare was sure Mahina's abilities would eventually surpass her own—and certainly those of Paoa.

But the reality was that Mahina hadn't completed her training. What happened in the day to come was uncertain. Tiare wasn't necessarily concerned about her own death—after all—she was ninety-five and had lived a full and rich life. But Mahina's death was an entirely different matter. Tiare loved her deeply and knew that the Rapanui would never recover from the enormous loss of a shaman to direct their spiritual paths.

Tiare thought about what it would be like to die. She wasn't at all afraid of death; she had walked the spiritual planes most of her long existence, and they felt familiar and comfortable. And she longed to share the heavenly realms with Ernesto, her husband who died many years ago. She loved him dearly and to spend precious moments with him exploring the Universe would be a dream come true.

Saint Paul had once said, "I die daily," and Tiare knew exactly what he had meant.

But, as she thought deeply about it, letting go of life wasn't quite as easy as it seemed, in spite of what some might say. *A richness and beauty comes with being in the body and experiencing its ups and downs.*

Tiare would miss the day-to-day interactions with those she loved. Not only that, also the little things that made life so precious: the cup of honeyed tea in the morning, the soft feel of the couch as she sat on it, the taste of fresh papaya just picked from the tree, the laughter of children, the fragrance of freshly cut peppermint. And, except for the Death Prayer, which had her in its devastating grip, Tiare had been quite spry, healthy, and enjoyed learning and growing.

As she thought about the approaching sunrise, possibly the last one of her life, she recalled a quote from the Sioux leader Crazy Horse, one Daniel had shared with her. He is reported to have once said, as battle approached, "Today is a good day to die."

Tiare angrily thought, as she clenched her fists in frustration, *No, today is not a good day to die. It can't be the time—it can't. There must be a solution.*

What is it?

Her mind drew a blank.

Tiare bowed her head and prayed with all the energy her weakened body and mind could muster.

Oh Divine Force that rules the Universe, help me.

Tears flowed from her eyes onto her cheeks.

Help me . . .

Please.

Chapter 23

Daniel arrived early in the afternoon at the train station of Haverfordwest. There, he discovered that most signs had the Welsh language word above the English version, so above Haverfordwest was *Hwlffordd*. He had no idea how to pronounce it.

He was not hungry, and the train had ample snacks for purchase. He had enjoyed some hot tea and *bara brith*—a traditional Welsh fruitcake made with self-rising flour, raisins, currants and candied peel.

Rental car obtained, he set out on the road. Sitting on the right side of the front seat was odd enough, but it was even stranger to drive on the left side of the road. After some moments of tedious driving, he adjusted and headed toward his destination, Carn Menyn.

Daniel had done some research on his laptop the night before. Carn Menyn, which actually means butter rock, is a rocky pinnacle of white-spotted dolerite rocks, perched high on the Preseli ridge, which many believed was the primary quarry for the Stonehenge bluestones. Others speculated that the Stonehenge bluestones came from a number of different places in Wales, including Pont Saeson, which Daniel planned to visit tomorrow.

As Daniel turned off the main highway, he discovered that the country roads were much narrower than those he was accustomed to. Not only that, the hedgerows—ancient fences that consisted of thick rows of mostly hawthorn and blackthorn—rose high above the road in many places, preventing a clear view of the countryside.

Despite the confusion, Daniel soon arrived at the point of entry to Carn Menyn, and he parked his car on the side of the dirt road. Biting cold and drizzling rain greeted him when he got out of the car. He zipped up his fleece jacket and put on his worsted wool hat. Shouldering his back pack, he set out.

He followed a gentle incline upward. The ground was muddy and rocky, and Daniel walked a zigzag course to avoid pools of standing water. To his left was a dense forest of cultivated trees, and to his right, a number of picturesque rolling hills surrounded by fields of farmland, bordered by hedgerows. To center himself, Daniel did a walking meditation, timing his breathing with his steps.

After an hour of slow, measured hiking, he arrived at Carn Menyn. The rocky outcropping was far more beautiful than the pictures he had seen.

Daniel climbed to the highest point, sat on a boulder and surveyed the countryside. Abruptly, he became aware of a presence above him. He looked up and discovered a beautiful sparrowhawk circling and screeching, as if to get his attention. Daniel waved at it, then closed his eyes. He straightened his back and focused on his breath. In his mind's eye, he began to appreciate a white glow around the rocks. Before long, a vision unfolded.

> Daniel saw large groups of prehistoric men, wearing animal hides and working with primitive wooden tools, removing large rocks from just below where he was sitting. Some of the bluestones shined brighter than others, and a woman dressed in a white animal skin seemed to know which ones they were. Those were selected out from the others, and the brightest ones were loaded on rollers and sledges, then pulled to the sea where they were placed onto rafts.
>
> In his vision, Daniel watched as the rafts made a precarious journey across the ocean, eventually landing at the mouth of the Avon River. From there, the bluestones were dragged to Stonehenge to join with the much larger sarsen stones, some of which were already upright.
>
> A blinding light flashed, and, all at once before him stood a completed Stonehenge. Its symmetry and beauty were astounding, and the light that

Daniel had previously detected around the stones was multiplied a thousandfold. The landscape had changed, though, and now a number of round barrows—heaps of earth placed over prehistoric tombs—were in close proximity.

After another flash of light, Daniel could see the sun rising in the northeast horizon. The morning sun beamed into the heart of Stonehenge, so Daniel knew he was seeing it on June twenty-first, the summer solstice, the longest day of the year. Thousands of men, women and children gathered at the mouth of the Avon River, weaving side to side with interlocked arms as they sang and ceremoniously approached Stonehenge from the Avenue, the curvilinear route from the river. Many of the women and girls had garlands of flowers around their necks, and some of the men had dead bodies wrapped in animal hides and secured with twine thrown over their backs.

The smell of burning flesh hung heavy in the air as the men threw the corpses into the large bonfires on the periphery of Stonehenge, and tears were in the eyes of many of the participants. Daniel could only guess that they were saying farewell to their loved ones, whose cremated bodies were being left behind in the most sacred temple of ancient England—Stonehenge.

With the passage of time, a huge crowd arrived, and they gathered around the glowing formation. A woman covered with a long, white animal hide, much like the one Daniel saw at Carn Menyn, stood in the center and raised her arms, which gradually brought the assembly to silence.

She spoke in a dialect which was English but hard for Daniel to understand. She proclaimed, "We gather here, not only to celebrate the lives of those who have passed on to the heavenly realms, but also to rejoice in the longest day of the year and the gifts that the summer brings us."

The crowd roared in approval.

"Soon," she continued, "we will make merry with feasting, dance and music."

Again, a cheer rose up.

"But now it is time for those who are ill to bathe in the healing light that our temple freely gives. For those of you who wish to do so, now is the time to enter."

A single file of pilgrims approached from the Avenue, some using crutches, others wearing crudely fashioned bandages. The ailing ones were directed by a group of men and women dressed in a similar fashion as the speaker. With what seemed their last bit of energy, they slowly strolled through the central part of the sacred rocks, soaking in the glow of the formation. Some threw down their crutches as they exited, but all had looks of ecstasy on their faces.

Daniel felt tears come into his eyes.

As the vision faded, Daniel thought, *What a holy place Stonehenge was!* He could see this ever so clearly. Gordon Green was right. The bluestones were brought from far away for their healing, restoring qualities. Stonehenge was far more than a place of ceremony, burial and celebration.

Stonehenge was a temple of healing.

When Daniel opened his eyes, a sparrowhawk, no doubt the one that had earlier circled over him, now sat on a boulder no more than five feet away.

Daniel silently asked, *Are you my spirit animal?*

In his mind, Daniel heard, *I am.*

Daniel again thought, *I sense you are not a member of my family.*

I am not. They have traveled on to other realms. I am your animal guide and will accompany you through the land of spirit when you have need. Have your questions been answered?

Yes.

Then you should know that you are in grave danger.--Quickly, to the ground!

What?

To the ground. Now!

The sparrowhawk flew at him, startling him off the boulder. At that moment, four gunshots rang out, the bullets ricocheting off the rock behind him. Daniel then heard rapid footsteps exiting the area. He dared not pursue; he had no weapon. But his assailant did not know that.

He heard the sparrowhawk's wings flap as it flew away. He lay on the ground for some time, face forward in the ice-cold mud.

Daniel would take his time before he got up.

Chapter 24

As the sun was just beginning to light the morning sky, Tiare lay on the couch, with Mahina seated on a chair across from her. Mahina held her hands just above Tiare's heart, palms down, and directed healing light into her.

Mahina was intense with concentration, but tears hung at the corners of her eyes; she was aware that Tiare was dangerously close to dying. When she had scanned Tiare's energy field just a few moments ago, Tiare's sluggish, dull green heart chakra had almost quit moving. The restoring force Mahina directed to her would buy some time, but not much.

Tiare was lethargic and moving in and out of consciousness. She could feel that her spiritual body was on the verge of leaving her aged form. The silver cord, the etheric connection that held her soul to her physical body, was beginning to thin. The moment her heart chakra ceased to function, the cord would snap apart and she would die.

With the treatment, Tiare roused and said, "Mahina—thank you. You have given me more time to live and breathe, and that is a great blessing."

Tears now freely flowed down Mahina's face. "Teacher, have you not discovered a way to rid yourself of this affliction?"

"I'm afraid not. My fate is now in the hands of the Divine."

Mahina only nodded. She couldn't bring herself to speak.

"My precious student, with your care I am able to talk again, and there are some important words I must share with you. First of all, your shaman apprenticeship is close to completion, but should I die now, and it seems likely, I want you to know of a Maori shaman in Auckland, New Zealand, named Anahera, who is a close friend of mine. Her name, address and phone number are listed in my address book, which sits on my bedside table. I have already spoken to her about you, and she is willing to continue and complete your training."

"Let's hope that's not necessary."

Tiare cracked a weak smile. "Thank you. Now, you should know I expect Paoa to attack at any time. I imagine his entrance to be impressive, to suit his amazingly large ego. Once you have finished with this treatment, I would like for you to sit in meditation, and the light you had previously directed to me, now turn toward yourself and soak every cell of your body with it. Prepare your inner resources so that you might be able to respond to whatever Paoa throws your way."

Mahina trembled as she whispered, "I will."

"I have thought about this and have but one warning: What is most important is for *you* to survive this attack, not me. Remember, I am ninety-five and have had a full life. What happens to me is of little importance."

"I don't believe that."

Tiare was insistent. "Mahina, I must have your promise, no matter what happens, to make yourself a priority. Do not be distracted by what occurs to me. I am confident that if you maintain your center and focus on defending yourself, you are capable of warding off any attack. If not, not only do you put yourself at risk but also future of the Rapanui people.

Tiare pleaded, "Now, do I have your promise?"

Mahina shook her head from side to side. "Teacher, I cannot..."

Tiare weakly murmured, "If you love me, and I know you do, honor this request. Please?"

Mahina openly wept. "Yes, teacher," she choked out, "I ... I will do ... as you wish."

"Good," Tiare whispered as she closed her eyes, "Now I can rest, knowing you are safe."

At that moment, a glowing red-and-black vapor oozed under the front door and into the room.

Mahina briefly closed her eyes, breathing in and out, centering herself. She then opened her eyes and watched as a form began to coalesce before the door.

As panic and fear threatened to overwhelm her, Mahina's thoughts went to Dan-iel.

My love, she fervently whispered, *I need your strength right now.*

Immediately, she felt a surge of courage.

Mahina was prepared—as much as anyone could be.

Chapter 25

Daniel was walking back down the hill from Carn Menyn when he had a strong feeling that Mahina and Tiare were in grave danger.

He immediately paused and directed love to them, taking his time, even as he stood in the cold, spitting rain. He held his palms up in front of him, sending them as much blessing and protection as he was capable of. He hoped it would help.

God, it has to, he thought. *What else can I do?*

He then refocused on his own situation and warily approached his car. He spotted no one close at hand. Next to the car, he could see the fresh tracks of another vehicle, but the rain was already washing away this potential identification.

Daniel checked the tires, and after he was certain they had not been slashed, hopped in and headed toward Newport, where he would check in at The Golden Lion Hotel, a family-run inn. Once in his room, he would call the local police, and no doubt he would have to return to Carn Menyn today to help with the investigation.

He hoped that bullets could be found, to see if they matched with those fired at Stonehenge and Salisbury. But in his heart, he knew confirmation wasn't necessary.

He was certain they did.

It was late in the evening when Daniel was able to return to The Golden Lion Hotel, appropriately painted a golden yellow color. He parked his rental car, and after receiving a friendly greeting at the front desk, slowly trudged up to his comfortable room on the second floor.

Daniel was exhausted and hungry, yet his mind was on overdrive. Not only was he concerned about Mahina and Tiare, but also his thoughts were scrambled and confused about the series of murders he had come to investigate. The number of variables was confounding. It amazed him that someone had come all the way to Wales to kill him, which he knew could only mean one thing:

I am getting close, and the killer knows that.

I am on the right track.

Before Daniel left the scene, two of the bullets had been found by the local police. Daniel was assured that they would immediately be flown by helicopter to Scotland Yard, where a rush would be put on the ballistics. Once completed, Inspector Green would be promptly notified.

After the day Daniel had undergone, he needed pleasantries, and The Golden Lion Hotel was the perfect place to receive them. He walked downstairs to the quiet hotel restaurant, where he was served a sumptuous dinner of wild-caught salmon, mashed potatoes, and steamed, buttered asparagus, topped off with a dessert of warm chocolate cake and ice cream.

Rested and sated, Daniel returned to his room and tried to call Mahina.

No answer.

He sighed, and after a long pause, pulled his laptop out of his backpack. With nothing more he could do about Mahina, he focused on the situation at hand. It was time to get some answers.

He first initiated a search on stones that were believed to have healing powers, such as bluestones. He discovered there was much information, most of which didn't make sense. But, just for fun, he decided to continue, free thinking as he went from site to site.

Okay, here's one place that says different astrological signs are benefitted by certain stones. Since I'm a Leo, I'll have a look. Here it states that pink topaz brings good luck to Leos, and rock crystal gives Leos balance and strength.

Hmm . . . pretty strange.

He found another site that claimed certain gemstones can increase the flow of energy to different chakras—points of spiritual power in the body. "Obtain a smooth, flat stone and lay it over the chakra for at least an hour a day to get the full benefit: a garnet for the first chakra, orange jasper for the second chakra," and so on.

Pretty interesting, but where's the science? Daniel was as open minded as anyone, but this was stretching things way too much for him.

He quieted his concrete mind and focused on his vision at Carn Menyn. He had no doubt that the bluestones had spiritual and healing qualities. He silently tipped his hat to Gordon Green, as he once again realized his theory had been right all along.

With a fresh outlook, he explored specific stones.

Amethyst? "Hildegard of Bingen had been successful in treating skin lesions with amethyst." Daniel had read a number of books written by her, and had always admired Hildegard, a composer, writer, Christian visionary and mystic—a woman of many talents.

Aventurine? "This stone was sewn into the battle garments of men going off to war to help maintain their courage." *I could have used some of that today,* Daniel thought with a smile.

Carnelian? "The Egyptians believed it gave them vitality and energy" . . . another stone praised by Hildegard of Bingen.

Emerald? "A stone associated with Mercury, the messenger of the Gods," it supposedly provides protection for travelers.

Daniel started to tire as he read about gemstone after gemstone, and the list never seemed to end. The night grew late, and he yawned.

Well, let me read about one more.

Shiva lingam? "A stone formed in the Namada River, high in the mountains of India. It has been termed the Stepping Stone to Enlightenment and has been reported to have healing properties."

This sounds a lot like the bluestone.

"This egg-shaped stone is a form of quartz called cryptocrystalline. This crystal has a higher vibration than any other natural stone on Earth" *How would they know that?* "It is used to cleanse emotional impurities in the home. The shiva lingam represents the highest power, the power of transformation that exists within each of us. This sacred stone stands for the balance and harmony of the soul as the Philosopher's Stone is born . . ."

What? It says what?

"The Philosopher's Stone," Daniel said aloud.

Daniel rubbed his eyes. He had been exhausted, but now he was buzzing with energy.

Surely this couldn't be, but . . . yet?

Was it possible?

He would call Gordon Green for help and would not visit Pont Saeson in the morning. He would enjoy seeing another source of the bluestones, but such a visit would have to wait. Tomorrow, he would be on the earliest train back to Salisbury.

The answer to the Stonehenge conundrum was—possibly—within his reach.

But the explanation was fraught with danger.

At last, he understood why the killer would stop at nothing, and that included murdering him and anyone else who threatened to get in the killer's way.

Daniel had to return to Salisbury immediately.

Before someone else is murdered.

Chapter 26

The glowing red-and-black vapor coalesced to form the fiery, smoky image of Paoa, standing just before the front door of Daniel and Mahina's home. Heat radiated from him.

Mahina could feel it from ten feet away.

Paoa glowered at the two women with murky, dark eyes, then broke into a malevolent sneer.

"Well, Mahina, we finally meet again. It's been a long time since you killed me in the time cave. As I was dying on the cold floor, I swore I'd get revenge, and, now, at long last, I have the chance." His voice erupted into a cackling laugh, and he stared at Tiare, who opened her eyes and looked helplessly at him.

He mocked Mahina, saying, "I'm so sorry to see your friend, the shaman Tiare, so hopelessly ill. The Death Prayer has not made her feel well—not at all." He paused to savor the sound of his words. "I have had two previous opportunities to kill her. But don't worry—as they say in your modern culture—the third time is a charm, and soon she will be dead and suffering no more. You do want to end her suffering, *don't* you?"

Mahina felt rage surging inside her, and despite the emanating heat from Paoa, started to move toward him.

"Angry, are we?" Paoa taunted. "Move a little closer so I can touch you and burn the skin off your beautiful face."

He watched her through narrowed eyes as she stopped. "Do you think *Dan-iel* would still love you if you were burned and ugly? Perhaps, but I think you would be wise to stay where you are. I have other plans for you."

Enjoying the moment immensely, he continued with a smirk on his face, "You see, I desire to do more than just burn your face. I want you to die first, so the image of your passing will be the last thing your mentor sees before the Death Prayer does its work."

Paoa exclaimed, "Now—be amazed at my power!" He lifted his arms above his head and the front door exploded into wooden shards. He faced outdoors and said, "Come to me, my beloved ones. Come now!"

Nothing seemed to happen for a few moments, but then an odd mixture of gurgling, sloshing and buzzing sounds approached from the distance. To Mahina's disgust, the odor of rotting flesh preceded a parade of carrion insects, flying and crawling through the doorway, the ones on the tiled floor leaving slime in their wake. Flies, maggots, worms of various shapes and colors, wasps, ants and necrophagous beetles gradually came inside. The heat from Paoa seemed not to affect them, and the insects crawled and flew onto and into him, turning Paoa into a solid, pitch-black mass of rolling, undulating waves of insects.

The cacophony of sounds mixed with the putrid smell were sickening, and Mahina fought to maintain her composure. *Nothing could have prepared me for this.* She glanced at Tiare, whose eyes were still open but glazed over. She was barely breathing.

"Do you remember, Mahina, when I had planned to eat Dan-iel's flesh and feel his *mana*—his power—inside me?"

Staring at him intensely, Mahina said nothing

"Oh, I'm sure you remember. How could you forget? Well, I have been waiting to do the same thing to you, but a question arose. How do I do it without a body? This was quite a puzzle, and I needed to do some dabbling in the darkest, most evil places. At long last, I found the answer.

"You see, my little friends here prefer dead flesh. But I have been given them the special ability to dine on living tissue. Mahina, you will be the first breathing person they will have eaten, and they will feast all the way down to your bones. They can have your body, but, in turn, I will receive your *mana*. A worthwhile trade, don't you think?"

Mahina dispassionately gazed at Paoa. His words did not frighten her; rather, they created greater defiance. She was keenly aware of her own inner strength. She despised him because of what he had done to Tiare.

She bristled and challenged him. "Come for me, if you dare."

Paoa chuckled and said, "Oh, I dare."

Now a solid mass of parasitic horror, he gradually worked his way toward Mahina, and his laughter became increasingly sinister.

Mahina had no fear. Just as Tiare had taught her, she pulled the healing light of the Universe inside her through the top of her head, and the energy field around her became vibrant and energetic.

Paoa continued to approach. Before he reached the edge of her aura, he paused and announced, "Your paltry efforts at protecting yourself will have no effect on me."

He then inched closer, barely touching Mahina's aura. A bright flash of light, along with a sizzling, popping sound like that of an electric shock, exploded from the area of contact. Paoa was thrown to the other side of the room and knocked to the floor. A pile of dead insects lay at his feet, and a charred, smoky smell filled the air.

Mahina glanced at Tiare, now completely comatose.

"Tiare?"

No response.

As Paoa shakily stood, a horde of insects entered through the doorway and once again made him a solid, buzzing, dark collection of putrid, squirming insects.

Mahina reluctantly focused her attention on Paoa, determined to stop him. *If I don't give Tiare a healing treatment soon*, she thought, *my teacher and friend will die.*

"It seems I have underestimated you," Paoa conceded. "Your teacher has taught you much in a short time, more than I could have imagined possible. I will have to change my plans."

Paoa delayed a moment for dramatic effect and said, "The old woman will die first."

He raised his right arm, pointed it at Tiare, and a beam of unearthly, red-tinged darkness burst from his index finger onto her.

The minute it hit, the old woman's eyes opened wide, her teeth clenched, and she paled and broke out into a sickly sweat. Mahina watched in anguish as Tiare slowly breathed in and out, appearing to fight the evil with every bit of the strength she had left.

Paoa intensified the hellish beam, and Tiare lurched from the impact.

"Die, old woman, *die*!" he yelled.

"I will never . . . yield . . . to you," Tiare somehow managed to say.

The flow of darkness from Paoa increased into a torrential river of evil, jolting Tiare once again. Even with the force of it, Tiare cracked a slight smile and said, "Is that the best . . . you . . . can do?" To Mahina's dismay, blood began to ooze from the corners of Tiare's eyes.

"Stop!" Mahina immediately redirected the dazzling bright light from herself to surround Tiare.

Tiare forcefully whispered to Mahina, "No! Remember your promise . . . you must protect *yourself*!" With those words, her eyes closed and she stopped breathing.

The warning came too late; in an instant, Paoa pointed both of his hands at Mahina and surrounded her with a sphere of gloomy darkness. Mahina tried to pull the light back down into herself, without result. Paralyzed, even her own breathing became difficult. She wobbled from side to side and found it difficult to stay on her feet.

Paoa teemed with voracious insects, as he slowly and patiently walked toward her, enjoying every second of his triumph. His face moved inches away from Mahina's. She felt her face burn from the heat.

The excited chatter of the insects increased. Their meal awaited them.

"Now my friends," Paoa said with a hiss. "Enjoy your feast."

Chapter 27

When Daniel arrived in Salisbury on the early afternoon train from Wales, Gordon Green met him at the station, once again wearing his green tweed three-piece suit, covered by an open black trench coat.

"DeWoody could not be here," Green said as he shook Daniel's hand. "He sends his apologies for his absence, but his superior sent him to Canterbury to assist with a dispute the constables there are facing."

"I understand. I'm glad to see you."

Green looked at Daniel quizzically. "I believe you have some interesting things to discuss."

"I do," Daniel replied. "Is there a place where we can talk privately?"

"Naturally. Let's load in my car and head to the Churchill Gardens, which is just south of the city center. Today has been unseasonably warm, and we can sit and chat by the river."

Once on their way, Green began to update Daniel. "Before you launch into your business, I have some news for you. I received a call from the Yard just a bit ago. The ballistics from your adventure in Wales match the bullets used in the killings here. I suppose you're not shocked by that?"

"Not at all."

"Also, remember the camera recordings you asked DeWoody to check into?"

"Yes, the ones from the night that Olga Alexeyeva died?"

"Exactly. A one-hour lapse exists in the recordings. We interviewed the monitor tech—George—and he confessed he fell asleep during that time."

"Too odd to be just a coincidence," Daniel said.

"We agree. We have already done a drug screen on him, and his urine was positive for benzodiazepines."

"The Valium, Xanax and Ativan family of drugs?"

"Right, and because George was on no medications, we assume the killer drugged his tea, turned off the cameras then borrowed George's employee badge for access to Alexeyeva."

"Does he have any idea who spiked his drink?

"Not a clue. It had been setting on his desk for a while, and several times during his shift he got up to go to the loo, so the drugging must have happened during one of those times."

"What about Mrs. Ambrose?"

"She was in another wing of the hospital when the recording interruption occurred. When she returned to the station, George had revived, the cameras were back on, and he was too embarrassed to say anything about what had happened."

"What do you think?" asked Daniel. "Outside or inside job?"

Green's eyes narrowed. "Hard to say. Any of the staff could have done it. As you know, the hospital is a large facility, and some one hundred employees worked that shift. And since hospital policy allows visitors twenty-four-hour access, it could have been anyone."

"Are there any cameras on the monitoring station? Could we see anyone go into his work station?"

Green shook his head. "I'm afraid not. The cameras are trained only on the hallways."

"What do you think about the Chanel Number Five I smelled in the room?"

"If you did, and I know you had some doubt, it would certainly point to an outsider. Very few who work there can afford perfume that expensive. Even if they can, they're not wearing it to work."

"How much does it cost in the UK?" Daniel asked.

"I don't believe you can find it for anything less than sixty-five pounds."

"So, it's expensive, but not financially inaccessible to the average person."

"Yes," Green confirmed.

Green pulled his police car into the car park area of the Churchill Gardens. They both stepped out and enjoyed a brief walk to some benches by the river. The wintered grass was dead and brittle, but the rippling water was beautiful as ducks swam back and forth across it. Birds soared overhead, and Daniel looked up, hoping he could once again see a sparrowhawk.

Green settled into his seat. "All right, what's on your mind?"

Daniel came right to the point. "You once told me that you enjoyed history, especially history that was unusual or mysterious."

"Right."

"What can you tell me about . . . alchemy?"

"Alchemy? Why in God's creation would you want to know about that?"

"Indulge me, please. I'll explain later."

"Very well . . . First of all, before I begin, tell what you know of it."

"Not much. Most scientists believe that alchemy is a pseudoscience, so I haven't spent much time studying it. I do know, historically speaking, that the goal of alchemy was to produce the Philosopher's Stone, which could be used to transmute base metals into gold."

"That's true. But there is much, much more. Alchemy, like Stonehenge, is one of my stronger areas of interest. Even though you are bloody smart, I likely know more about it than you."

"Probably," Daniel said, sardonically.

Green chuckled. "Let's start from the beginning. Do you know what the definition of alchemy is?"

"Doesn't it have something to do with change?"

"Actually, *transformation*—alchemy is the art of transformation. Alchemists attempt to convert something that is flawed into something purer and closer to perfection. The process could be about changing lead into gold, preparing herbal tinctures, or improving the body, mind or spirit. It encompasses all these subjects and more."

"I see. Since you're a historian, what is the background of alchemy?"

Green squinted a bit. "That is a complicated topic, but I'll try to condense it as best I can. Legend tells us that the roots of alchemy began in Egypt during a period known as the Zep Tepi, some twelve thousand years ago, when a group of godlike beings took residence in Egypt."

Daniel interrupted, "Mythology?"

"Yes," Green confirmed. "One of those beings was Thoth, who had the body of a man and the head of an ibis—a tall wading bird. Thoth was the creator of writing and language, and is considered to be the founder of many fields of study, including mathematics, science, medicine and, of course, alchemy. He is said to have written a number of books, though the best known one was the Emerald Tablet, a compendium of alchemical tenets."

"If he was real, he would have been a genius."

"Agreed." Green concurred with a grin. "Putting all this aside, the first known alchemy books surfaced in China, Mesopotamia and Egypt sometime close to two thousand years ago, and many historians believe that the origins of alchemy actually began during that period. Alchemy flourished in Asia and Arabia and at long last became known in Europe with the Arabian invasion of Spain. It spread from there to the rest of the world."

Daniel asked, "Can you help me understand more about the Philosopher's Stone?"

"As you mentioned, alchemists believe the Philosopher's Stone is the means through which base metals can be transmuted to gold, but it could also be used to produce remedies that can rejuvenate the body. They also thought the Philosopher's Stone had the potential to catalyze the transformation of the spiritual self to obtain enlightenment."

"How was it actually made?"

"Ah, Hawk, you ask a most interesting question. If I knew, I'd be producing one myself. As claimed by alchemical writings, there is a wet way and a dry way. The wet way, which utilizes organic methods, is safer in its approach. The dry way, which works much faster, utilizes extreme temperatures and potent chemicals. Both are reported to produce a Philosopher's Stone, but, for those who chose the dry way, there is the risk of insanity."

Daniel's caught his breath. "Ian Johansen and Olga Alexeyeva?"

Green glanced at Daniel in disbelief, uncomfortably cleared his throat and went on without answering. "In alchemy, three classic stages are necessary for the production of a Philosopher's Stone. The first, the black phase, happens when base metals, such as tin, iron, copper and lead, are liquefied and joined into a black alloy. The white phase comes when this alloy is refined and the essences split apart from any residual impurities. The last part, the red phase, occurs when the forces that are set free from the black and white phases are placed in a powder or solution."

"It sounds fairly cookbook to me," Daniel said.

"It's not as simple as it sounds. I have only given you the basics, and, remember, alchemy is more than just a physical practice, it's a spiritual one as well."

"I see."

"Anyway, as I was saying, if one chooses to perform the red phase using the dry way, some red coloring may form on the top of the melted product. This is symbolized by the phoenix."

Daniel almost fell off the park bench. "What did you say?"

"The phoenix," Green repeated. "I say, Hawk, why do you appear so gobsmacked? You look like a bloody shambles."

"I'll explain later . . . I will . . . but first I'd like to learn more about alchemy," Daniel said as he took a moment to compose himself. "All of this sounds interesting in theory, but has anyone actually made a Philosopher's Stone?"

Green sighed. "A number of anecdotal reports exist about the creation of a Philosopher's Stone, but no scientific substantiation can be found."

"Do any of these accounts say what a Philosopher's Stone actually looks like?"

"Well, it was reportedly dark red in color, had a jagged form and the appearance of glass crystal. Also, there's a rather odd legend that it has a variable weight, could be as heavy as a brick of lead or as light as air."

Daniel felt the intensity rising and questioned, "I have read that the shiva lingam stone found in India can help in precipitating the Philosopher's Stone. Have you heard of that?"

"That would be news to me," Green said, offhandedly. "I've not heard that before. Now, enough questions. Hawk, tell me what this is all about. What does alchemy have to do with anything related to these murders?"

"Don't you see? It all adds up. Around twenty years ago, someone here in Salisbury—who, I don't know—decided to embark on a mission to create a

Philosopher's Stone. The brightest minds from various international locales were invited to join, and, eventually, they combined into a small consortium in Salisbury, with the goal of creating one."

Chief Detective Green stared at Daniel without a hint of what he was thinking.

"Then," Daniel went on, "after years of fruitless struggle, the breakthrough occurred when one of the members of the group discovered that the shiva lingam stone had been used in Indian alchemy to catalyze the production of a Philosopher's Stone. So, the group members thought they'd try another sacred stone, a bluestone from Stonehenge, which was a resounding success, and the long awaited Philosopher's Stone became a reality. More gold than the group could ever imagine was created.

"But greed reared its ugly head. Either one of the members of the group, or perhaps an outsider who became aware of their schemes, began to kill off members of the elite consortium, one by one, to obtain their gold. Think about it. Why would the killer go to so much trouble to conceal the contents of the safes? There's only one answer: If a detective investigating the case discovered gold was in all of them, that would potentially raise suspicions.

"Besides," Daniel gulped and added, "I've had a dream about the phoenix."

Green looked dumbfounded. "Blimey, Hawk. A dream?"

"Yes, a dream."

Green said, "So, what should we do now?"

"I don't know. Somehow, we must discover who the organizer is. Once we know that, I believe the answers will fall into place."

Green sat silently for a long time, staring at the ducks as they crisscrossed the water. Finally, he blurted out, "Hawk, what you suggest is bloody insane!"

"But it's the only thing that makes sense, don't you agree?"

"In some odd way, it does, but can you imagine what would happen if we presented your idea to my superiors? I'd be fired faster than you can say 'boo,' and I'd be the laughingstock of Scotland Yard. So much for my reputation, my retirement and all I've worked for over the years.

"I'm sorry Hawk, but you're on your own on this one. You will have my silent but not my verbal support in your investigation. If someone gets wind of what you are doing and reports you, I will denounce you and have you removed from the case.

You will be sent back home to Easter Island like a punished dog with your tail between your legs. Have I made myself clear?"

"Yes." *Crystal clear.*

"Good. Let's go find a car so you can be mobile for the investigation."

Green stood, followed by Daniel, and they silently walked back to the car.

Daniel parked his rental car in front of the Salisbury Bed and Breakfast and sat for awhile to think. As much as he hated to admit it, Green was right. This was the most ludicrous, harebrained idea Daniel had ever come up with, and he couldn't expect Green to risk everything to join forces with him.

But Daniel knew he was headed in the right direction—no other answer fit. The answer lay in finding out who the ringleader was, but he had no idea where to begin. Somehow, someway, Daniel believed there was a clue he had missed, one that would give him the answer he needed.

But what is it?

Daniel got out of the car and walked through the front door of the bed and breakfast. There to greet him in the reception area was James Trueblood, wearing a long-sleeved burgundy sweater over a white dress shirt and khaki trousers. As Daniel shook James' hand, he was virtually slapped in the face by the strong odor of something that smelled like bleach.

Noticing his expression, James said, "Today is what Emily calls D-Day—Decontamination Day—when she goes over every inch of the house with a disinfectant called Domestos. Besides, she was bloody upset last night because some guests arrived who were picking their noses and not using tissues. She's cleaned everything at least three times over."

As if on cue, Emily popped out from around the corner, wearing a bright red dress with a white apron. Like before, the buttons of her dress were stressed and looked like they could snap off any minute. She wore a surgical mask and disposable blue-latex gloves. With a rag in one hand and a spray bottle in the other, every two to three seconds a volley of sprays and near-frantic wiping occurred.

"Beastly," she said. "Beastly!" She glanced over at Daniel. "Oh, good afternoon, Hawk."

"Hello," Daniel said.

"You'd think," she exclaimed, "that visitors would show better manners than to dirty up every square inch of our home. Especially with boogers!"

"You'd think." Daniel fought off the urge to roll his eyes.

Emily pushed past the two men, shrieking every now and then as she discovered a place, in her mind at least, that was grimy.

"Hawk, would you like to join me for a cuppa?" James had a flustered look on his face.

"A spot of tea? I'd love to." Daniel turned to join James.

The two men left Emily behind and walked into the dining area. James motioned for Daniel to be seated as he prepared the tea.

"Helluva thing about Ned. I'm guessing you've heard about it?" James said as he poured

"Thanks, James. Yes, I have," Daniel said as he placed both hands around his cup. "It was certainly a tragedy. What do you know about Ned?"

James sighed. "I'm familiar with him. When he was a young boy, for a number of years he delivered our papers. He was always so punctual and polite, 'Yes, sir,' 'No, sir.' Well, I think you get the picture."

"I do."

"I've never seen a smarter lad. He was first in his class in upper school. He always wore a black tie in those days, and some might have described him as a bit of a nerd. His parents were so proud of him when he was accepted with total funding at Cambridge. I suppose you've heard what happened to his parents?"

"I have."

"Then you know they were killed in a car accident—happened when he was at the university. Since he was an only child, their deaths were a devastating blow for him. But somehow he found a way to carry on, and he graduated with honors from Cambridge. He then found a job with a local pharmaceutical company and was their top research scientist. He was always well dressed and mannerly—until about three years ago, when his life spiraled downhill."

"What do you believe happened to him?"

"No one knows for sure. Ned was a quiet man with few friends, but local gossip said he had a love affair that went sour, and he became depressed. Since he had no family, if what they say is true, such a loss would be bloody difficult to handle on one's own."

"James, you've lived here all of your life and seem to know a lot about people in Salisbury. What can you tell me about Mrs. Ambrose?"

"The nurse who works at the mental hospital?"

"She's the one."

"She also grew up in Salisbury in a good family. She went to nursing school and landed her first job at the local hospital. She met her husband when she was taking care of him. He was a bit of a ruffian and had broken his jaw in a barroom brawl. It's hard to imagine why she married him; it's a classic case of how opposites attract. She was quiet and unassuming, yet he was loud and brash. I don't know this for fact, but talk has it he hits her every now and then when he's had too much to drink. Even though they're married, rumor has it he plays around with women who hang out at his favorite bar, The Velvet Peacock."

Daniel silently remembered the poorly concealed bruise he noticed under her eye when he visited the hospital.

James went on, "Later, she changed jobs to work at the Healing Mind and Spirit Hospital, likely just to get away from all the rumors swirling around her at her first place of employment."

James shifted subjects and asked, "By the way, are you making any progress on the investigation of these murders?"

"I'm sorry, James, but I can't say anything at this time. I hope you understand."

"I do. I just want to put the one responsible for this behind bars. He shouldn't be allowed to hurt others anymore. I don't care who he is. No one has the right to take the life of another."

Daniel nodded his agreement as he heard the swing of the pendulum of the hall clock. He then stood, saying, "James, I'd like to stay and chat with you longer, but, for now, I must get upstairs to my room. Is it the same one I had?"

"Yes," James fumbled in his pocket. "We saved it for you. We didn't think you'd be gone long. Here's your key."

"Good." Daniel took it from James. "I have work to do. Once I can tell you details about this nasty business, I will answer your questions, okay?"

"Ace!" James grinned broadly.

"Ace? What does that mean?"

"That's the British way of saying 'very good.'"

"Ace!" Daniel repeated with gusto.

They grinned at each other, shook hands again, then Daniel walked up the stairs to his room. He needed some time alone for reflection. Daniel thought about James' words. He was right.

The killer has to be stopped—now.

Daniel eased into the chair in his room. He kept his spine straight, closed his eyes and listened to his breath. After an hour or so, he felt centered and able to focus. He slowly and methodically replayed every scene since he had been in the UK. Moment by moment, he scanned every detail of every picture that moved across his mind. His thoughts were like a motion picture, playing frame by frame, and he took his time with each.

After a few hours, he reached a scene with a certain edginess and uneasiness to it. *Something did not fit.* Daniel patiently examined the picture in his mind.

Suddenly he had it.

Daniel went to his laptop and searched online. Sure enough . . . He wanted to yell, *Eureka!,* just as the old miners did when they discovered a vein of gold.

Daniel realized, though, he still had much to do. He stood from his chair, grabbed his coat and dashed out of the room, slamming the door behind him. If he acted quickly, he could solve the mystery tonight, when the dark of the new moon cloaked the surroundings.

Daniel jumped into his car and headed out.

He had not a second to spare.

Chapter 28

Mahina braced herself for the dreaded bites of the insects when she felt something crawl onto her shoulder. She turned her head and saw a gecko, its tongue flitting in and out, snapping up and gobbling down any insect that dared come too close to her.

Paoa angrily yelled, "How in the hell did that lizard get in here?" Stretching his hand forward, he reached for it.

Suddenly, the gecko opened its mouth and blue flame shot out—*whoosh!*—burning off the hand of Paoa and the insects of which it was composed.

"Ye-ouch!" Paoa screamed out. "How can that hurt? This is a spiritual body, not a physical one!"

Just as Paoa focused on his arm, a bare-chested Rapanui man, with long, tangled grey hair and an insane look on his face came out of nowhere and stood at Mahina's side. He smirked at Paoa and said, "It hurt, you idiot, because I wanted it to. Good job, Spirit!"

The gecko chirped and jumped from Mahina's shoulder onto his.

"Who are you?" Paoa stared at the wild man in disbelief.

"My name is Roberto Ika," he said, as brilliant blue fire flew from his hands, disintegrating all the remaining insects on and around Paoa. The ones about to enter the home scurried away.

Mahina cried more than yelled to Roberto. "Tiare—help her!"

Roberto took only an instant to pull a translucent violet rope out of thin air. He wrapped it tightly around Paoa, head to toe, gagged his mouth and pushed him to the floor. He then knelt down by Tiare, who was starting to turn blue.

Roberto checked for a neck pulse then shook his head from side to side.

"Quick!" he demanded of Mahina. "You are a healer. Direct the light to her!"

Mahina concentrated with all her being. The gleaming light shot from her hands with an incredible force. She simultaneously scanned Tiare's chakras.

No activity . . . anywhere.

Tears flowed as she continued her work. Minutes passed—no response.

Roberto looked with compassion at Mahina. "Stop," he asked.

"Why?" Mahina said, her hands still above Tiare.

"I'd like to try."

Mahina reluctantly pulled back as Roberto stepped in between Mahina and Tiare. He put his hands over the aged shaman.

"I see," he said.

"What?" Mahina questioned.

"Three captive spirits are still present in her body, the ones that Paoa enslaved to kill her with the Death Prayer."

"What can you do?" Mahina's voice was edged with panic.

"They must be convinced to leave; otherwise, any healing you perform will not be effective."

Roberto took several deep breaths and closed his eyes for a few moments.

Mahina felt desperate and wished he would hurry. Tiare looked worse with each passing moment.

Robert pronounced, in a powerful, yet kind way, "Souls in the body of Tiare—*hear me*! You have been enslaved by an evil one and forced to carry out a hex on a woman who does not deserve to die. You should know the wicked being is now no longer able to harm or control you. So, *listen!* I release you from your bondage. Leave now and go in peace."

A moment passed before a cool gust of breeze brushed their faces. Three ethereal balls of light spiraled up to the heavens, exiting through Tiare's solar plexus.

"It is done," Roberto sighed as he backed away. "Now, direct your light once more."

Mahina stepped forward and again put her hands over Tiare, sending love and healing radiance to her.

Nothing happened.

"Try again," urged Roberto.

Mahina trembled as once again, she flooded Tiare's chakras with restorative energy.

Tiare remained motionless, as did her chakras, and now her skin was an even darker blue color.

"Is she dead?" Mahina whispered.

"No," Roberto said. "May I help?"

"Please."

Once again, Roberto moved forward and placed his hands, palms down, next to Mahina's. He closed his eyes, and, together, they flooded Tiare with healing light.

After what seemed to Mahina to be an eternity, Tiare's chest began to slowly move up and down. Mahina put her hands over her mouth and gasped, as tears welled in her eyes.

Roberto grinned from ear to ear, shook his fists in front of him and exclaimed, "Yes!"

Tiare remained unconscious, but Mahina was able to feel a strong pulse in her neck.

Once Mahina regained her composure, she asked, "Roberto, why wasn't I able to heal her, once you rid her of the captive spirits?"

"It was important for you to know, no matter how skilled you are at something—and you are *very* skilled at healing—every now and then you might need a little help. It's okay to ask."

Mahina nodded.

"Besides," he continued, "I knew it wasn't yet Tiare's time to die. She still has work to do."

"Such as?"

"Finishing the training of our shaman-to-be. And, maybe, just maybe, she might be able to help you and Daniel sort out another crime or two."

"All of us?"

"Yes. In the days to come, I suspect you'll be much more than just a shaman. You have a gift for understanding the mysterious."

Mahina glanced over at Paoa, who struggled against his bonds, Mahina asked, "What should we do with him?"

"I think it's time he was sent on, out of this reality and into the Otherworld. There, he will be watched closely and he will no longer be able to reach into his bag of evil tricks. Would you like to help me?"

"I'd love to."

Roberto and Mahina both sat down in chairs, and, after a few moments of deep breathing, shimmering light beings that were their spiritual bodies stood beside their sitting forms.

Mahina walked beside Roberto as he picked up a still-struggling Paoa. Together, they strolled in silence until they reached a cluster of light beings that waited for them.

"The big boys and girls are here for this one," Roberto whispered.

Paoa fought against his spiritual shackles even harder, but every movement tightened them even more.

A large presence stepped forward, his arms extended in front of him. Roberto handed Paoa over to the entity, who wordlessly said, *At this soul's core is a beautiful being who became misguided. He, like all of us, has a radiant spark of God at his center. We will help him to realize that, once again. But, for now, I promise you, he will never disturb any of you again—ever.*

A brilliant, blinding white light issued from the being, and, when it faded, the spiritual bodies of Roberto and Mahina stood alone.

After a short hike, they stepped back through the shattered remnants of the front door and re-entered their sitting bodies. They opened their eyes and pulled both of their chairs, side by side, to face Tiare, who now rested comfortably on the couch.

Mahina now viewed Roberto with a new understanding, bringing back Tiare's words about him from so long ago.

She said to Roberto, "Thank you."

"Thanks are not necessary," he said. He bowed and added, "It was my pleasure."

They both sat and watched Tiare breathe.

Quite a beautiful sight.

Chapter 29

After Daniel's meditations revealed the leader of the clandestine group, he rushed to a local electronics store. He arrived just before it closed, and purchased a GPS—Global Positioning System.

Green had said he was on his own, so Daniel placed a call to the home of an old friend at the NYPD—one with British connections—and he covertly looked up the tag number needed to identify the leader's car. Daniel promptly drove to the suspect's place of employment and attached a tracker in a magnetic case to the bottom of the suspect's vehicle.

From there, he returned to the bed and breakfast, sat in front of his computer and waited. Before too long, the monitor showed movement, and, almost twenty kilometers out of town, the vehicle stopped and stayed for close to three hours. Daniel marked the location carefully and compared it to a topographical map he had purchased. He determined that the serpentine road leading to the hidden location went from the main road about one kilometer through a heavily wooded area. In spite of the woods, which can cause trouble for tracking devices, the signal was clear.

Just before ten p.m., the vehicle began to move again and, after a fifteen minute drive, ended at a location Daniel knew to be the home of his suspect. After it stayed in that location for the next hour, Daniel decided it was time to move in. He left his room and walked toward the front door. At the entry desk sat the cheerful Lily, wearing a stylish forest-green silk dress.

"Working late tonight?" Daniel asked as he approached the desk.

"Too late!" She feigned exasperation, hand held to her brow.

"Would you do me a favor, please?"

"Certainly."

He handed her a sealed envelope with "Chief Inspector Gordon Green" printed on the front. Inside, Daniel had placed directions to the suspected lair of the experimenters. He said to Lily, "If, for whatever reason, I don't return tonight, please make sure this is placed in Inspector Green's hands in the morning."

"I would be glad to," she said, placing the envelope in the top drawer of the desk.

Daniel then walked out the front door into the brisk night air. He looked at his watch just before he stepped in his car: 12:04 a.m. He left the bed and breakfast in a cold, sleeting rain to search for the secret location of the grand experiment, the place where he guessed the legendary Philosopher's Stone had been created. Daniel chose the late hour to avoid members of the secret consortium, who he hoped had finished for the day and had gone home.

A half-kilometer from the entry road to his destination, Daniel found a narrow dirt road that veered into the woods—a perfect place to conceal his car. He drove onto the road and parked under two over-arching trees. After locking it, he zipped up his black waterproof jacket, pulled the hood over his head and sloshed through pools of muddy, icy water, back to the highway. In less than ten minutes, he found the road leading to his destination. No gate obstructed it, which came as no surprise. Gates signal properties of those who wish to protect something, and a security gate would have aroused suspicion, exactly what the consortium did not want.

Daniel moved surreptitiously through the damp growth along the side of the road, hoping no one was still at the site, but readied himself to leap into the underbrush, just in case. He wished he had his weapon with him, but none of his fellow British detectives carried a gun, in spite of the risk, and except for the time when he was a target at Carn Menyn, he never felt in danger while in the UK.

Until now.

The night was dark—pitch dark—and Daniel used his keen eyesight to pick his way along, knowing he could not use the small LED flashlight he had bought at the electronics store. Compared to the blackness in the time cave on Rapa Nui, though, this hike was like walking on a sunny beach.

After a while, he approached a cleared section, and, even in the dark, he could see the faint outline of a parking area in front of a very large, paved slab—at least two acres in size—with air vents protruding above it. As he looked closer, Daniel spotted a flight of stairs leading down to an entry door. He overcame his initial puzzlement when he realized he was looking at a huge building: earth-sheltered and primarily subterranean.

Is someone there?

He had no way to know. But with no cars present, the odds were in his favor.

It was time to find a way inside.

Lily sat at the front desk of the bed and breakfast, waiting for the expected clients to arrive. They were hours late. She'd stood by many times before and had brought along some reading material when she came to work that morning. Lily loved fashion, and she had with her some of her favorite magazines: *Elle, Harper's Bazaar, Cosmopolitan* and *Vogue*. She enjoyed being with people and loved her job at the bed and breakfast but wanted to someday be a model and strut down a Paris runway, showing off the latest fashions, cameras flashing nonstop. She could just picture herself wearing the perfect clothes, the perfect makeup, smiling some—but not too much—after all, some degree of coyness was important in a good model.

All she needed to get her start was a break of some kind, and she hoped that would come tomorrow, when she had scheduled an afternoon audition in London with one of the top modeling agencies in the world, Models 1. Sure, Lily was a slender, petite woman, without the height of classic models, but hadn't Twiggy been?

No, nothing is in my way.

She believed she would land a position, and her dreams would come true.

Lily pulled a mirror from her purse, just to admire her flawless complexion. She mimicked her coy look, the one she had worked on for years. *How could the modeling executives resist?* They couldn't. She marveled at her sparkling blue eyes and naturally thick, black eyelashes, when she caught a hint of some unexpected movement behind her. She turned but saw nothing.

I must be imagining things.

She turned back to the mirror and smiled deeply, and two adorable dimples formed on both cheeks. She giggled with excitement. Then she heard a shuffling sound from close behind.

Lily gasped, but before she could turn around, two bullets entered the back of her head from close range, exiting through her once-perfect face. She fell, instantly dead, out of her chair and onto the floor.

Daniel slowly followed the road around the perimeter of the underground building. On the opposite side of the building, the road inclined downward to a loading dock, at least twenty feet below ground level. A large, corrugated metal entry door into the building was closed.

This is where they brought the Stonehenge bluestone into the research lab.

He walked back around to the front and pondered the best way of entry. He figured there was a standard security system, likely put in place around twenty years ago, one he could disable. No doubt the alarm would be set to sound to a member of the consortium, not to a monitoring company. Like the absence of a high-tech gate out front, the installation of an advanced protection system would arouse curiosity, so Daniel guessed the final layer of defense would be the safe itself, which could be purchased at another location and placed in the building away from probing eyes. Like the victims' homes, this facility relied on subterfuge rather than technology.

His heart pounded in his head. Daniel made his decision and walked down the steps to the front entry. If his guess was wrong, the end would come quickly. The experimenters would be on him like a fly on crap, and he wouldn't have a prayer of getting out alive. He walked down the steps to the front door, and on it were painted the words, *Ora et Labora*, Latin for "Pray and Work." Daniel remembered from his readings that this was one of the mottoes of alchemy. If he had any doubts about the correctness of his course, they were now dashed.

Daniel pulled a lock pick from his pocket, his LED flashlight from his belt, and, after a period of intense concentration, the door snapped open. Daniel slipped inside and discovered the alarm pad located on the wall inside the door, chiming its warning beeps. He replaced the pick and pulled out his wire clippers. Daniel snapped off the alarm casing and tediously snipped the appropriate wires, easily discernible under the glow of his flashlight. He waited, and, after the warning beeps stopped, no audible alarm sounded. Daniel knew there could have been a silent alarm, but he was sure he had already disabled it.

He pointed the flashlight ahead of him. He started into the room when he heard the click of pistol's hammer being pulled into position. Daniel turned around.

Standing before him was Doctor Siegfried Kratz.

"Hawk, welcome to our laboratory," he said, gun pointed at Daniel's head.

Chapter 30

When Tiare finally woke from her stupor, she discovered Mahina and Roberto seated beside her, with Spirit perched contentedly on Roberto's shoulder. They were smiling their biggest smiles, though Mahina still had tears in the corners of her eyes.

"Welcome back," Mahina said.

Tiare shook her head, trying to clear the cobwebs. She sat up and asked, "What happened? Mahina, the last thing I remember, Paoa was about to attack you."

"Roberto and Spirit arrived in the nick of time and rescued us from Paoa's clutches. We will have time for details later, but, for now, I must say that Roberto has taught Spirit some amazing skills."

Spirit happily chirped in confirmation.

Tiare scanned the room, looking from side to side. "Where is Paoa?"

Roberto answered, "We have escorted him to the Otherworld. We have been told by the powers-that-be that he will never trouble us again."

"Good," Tiare said, relaxing. "I wish him well on his journey. Directed in the proper way, Paoa could be a great force for good."

Mahina held her tongue. After seeing her friend and mentor nearly killed by Paoa's evil doings, she could not be so gracious. Besides, he had previously tried to kill Dan-iel. She could not forgive him—yet—and, for now, she wasn't ready to.

Tiare went on. "Now I can no longer sense the presence of the captive spirits in my body. I feel weak, but the numbness of my legs is no longer there. How were they dislodged?"

Mahina said, "Roberto was able to convince them to leave."

Tiare looked at Roberto incredulously. "How? I tried and tried to enter the dark place where the hex originated from so that I might learn the answer myself, but I was unable to pierce it."

"Dark?" Roberto raised his eyebrows. "You call that dark? I've been in places so black and murky that it makes the location of the Death Prayer look as innocent as a newborn baby. I brushed aside the resistance to my entry and was able to discover the secret words, and the right way to say them, that would release the entities from inside you."

But how did you know of our difficulty?" Mahina asked. She had been amazed when Roberto appeared, just in time.

"Didn't you hear me tell Daniel that I would keep an eye on things? After he left, I placed a small part of my consciousness on alert so I might know if you were having any problems. I sensed early on that there was an entity that wished both of you harm, but I chose not to interfere until it was clear you needed my help. Besides, Mahina, if Paoa had not tricked you by striking out at Tiare and forcing you to drop your guard, you never would have needed any assistance. I am certain that, one-on-one, Paoa wouldn't have had a chance against you."

Mahina sighed as the seeming weight of the Universe lifted from her shoulders. She had believed she was a failure. "Thank you, Roberto."

"I speak the truth," Roberto said.

Mahina smiled her appreciation. "I have a question for you."

Seeing Roberto's nod, she continued, "You seem so, please forgive me for the way this sounds—*sane*—right now, compared to how I have seen you before. What happened?"

Roberto laughed, which helped break the tension. "You see, Mahina, by most people's definition, I am crazy—my diagnosis is paranoid schizophrenia—and, because of that, sometimes I am unable to shut down the voices that come into my mind from the world of spirit. In these moments, it is hard to know the difference between ordinary and extraordinary reality. Most of the time, I am firmly centered in this world, such as now, but moments occur when I am not. When others see that behavior, I am labeled insane. In the past, this judgment bothered me, but nowadays I just grin and continue on. Certainly, I'm a better person because of what I've experienced, and I've learned not to judge *any* situation or *any* person."

"I understand," Mahina said.

"Not even Paoa." Roberto winked at her.

Mahina pondered his words. "You're right—not even Paoa. Now, since our danger is past, let us focus on Dan-iel. I've been most concerned about him lately. Tiare, can you tell me how he is doing?"

Tiare closed her eyes and breathed deeply, while Mahina and Roberto did the same. Suddenly, Tiare's eyes popped open, and she gasped. She took Mahina's hand and whispered to them, "Daniel is in grave danger. Hold him in an envelope of love and protection—*now*!"

Mahina gripped Tiare's hand and held it tightly. She thought, *Dan-iel—please be safe . . .*

I love you.

Chapter 31

Doctor Kratz lowered the gun to point at Daniel's chest. "Hawk, in case you were wondering, I found your little device under my vehicle. I left it at home and came here, hiding my car in a secret place. When you arrived, I was ready for you. But before I go on, I must admit my curiosity. I thought I had disguised myself quite well. How did you know?"

Daniel looked the doctor in the eye and said, "It wasn't easy."

"Yes?"

"Remember when I was in your office?"

"How could I forget?"

"Of the pictures on the wall, two of the three fit in quite well. Sigmund Freud and Hermann Rorschach were both prominent psychiatrists, but Paracelsus was different. He was not a doctor of the mind, and while a very important figure in early medicine, he was also known as a prominent alchemist, which is why I suspect you had his picture hanging in your office."

Doctor Kratz sighed. "So you figured out the purpose of our group. I underestimated you, Hawk. But it really doesn't matter; soon you will be dead. But before you die, would you like to have a little tour of our laboratory?"

"Sure," Daniel said, knowing anything to stall for time would be the right decision.

Kratz reached behind him and switched on the lights.

In front of Daniel stretched a very large, rectangular hallway, which appeared to be more like a library than a laboratory. Daniel caught his breath as he saw, in the exact center of the hall, the magnificent Stonehenge bluestone.

"Beautiful, isn't it?" said Kratz.

Daniel could only nod in amazement, but, at the same time, the stone seemed out of place so far from its sisters. When Daniel was finally able to look away from the bluestone, he noticed the walls were all paneled with dark-stained wood, as was the ceiling. Closed doors lined each side, which Daniel guessed were entries to individual laboratories. He was surprised to see, positioned right in front of him and Doctor Kratz, prayer benches placed before pictures of saints and sages of different religions.

Following Daniel's eyes, Kratz commented, "That place is called an *oratorium*. All of the researchers are required to spend time here in meditation and reflection before beginning their work for the day. As you may know, alchemy is a curious synthesis of spirit and science, and to ignore the spirit would have doomed our experiments to failure."

You're brutally killing people, thought Daniel, *and you think a little contemplation will compensate for that?*

For now, though, he kept silent. He glanced to the opposite end of the room, where two huge, silver-gray safes sat, so big and bulky that Daniel wondered how they'd been maneuvered into the building. Off to the left ran another large hallway, which Daniel supposed led to the loading dock.

Kratz asked, "Can you guess what is in those safes?"

Daniel didn't need to think long. "One must contain the gold you have produced . . . and the other must hold . . . the Philosopher's Stone?"

"Very good, Hawk. As the original organizer of this group, only I know their combinations. The technology is the best that money can buy, and it would be virtually impossible to crack them." Kratz waved his pistol at Daniel as he said, "Walk ahead of me, and I will show you one of our laboratories."

They stopped at the first door on their right. As Daniel stepped in, the potent smell of rotten eggs and vinegar shot up his nose. He briefly choked, then looked over to the left side of the room and discovered the odor's source—a large vat, nearly overflowing with black, bubbling fluid.

"What the hell?" Daniel blurted out without intending to. "That smell was the same one present—though barely detectable—at the crime scenes. No doubt it had clung to the killer's clothes."

Kratz chuckled. "You can see why we keep this door closed. The main purpose of this room is for the fermentation process of the wet way. I assume you've heard of it?"

"I have." Daniel noted the walls were lined with shelves that held glassware, pottery and utensils of all shapes and sizes. Stainless steel work tables were positioned nearby, and atop them were Bunsen burners, along with racks of glass beakers and test tubes, which contained different brightly colored fluids.

"As alchemists," Kratz said, "many varied types of glass vessels and earthenware are necessary for our experimental procedures, which include distilling, heating, separating and mixing, along with other operations."

Daniel saw numerous bottles of chemicals, stacked irregularly on the shelves, the print on a few being just large enough for him to read: ammonium chloride, green vitriol, oil of sulfur, liquor hepatis, pulvis solaris. Daniel had no knowledge of how these chemicals were used in alchemy, but if he somehow lived through this, he was determined to learn.

At the other end of the room stood a large brick oven, from which heat emanated.

"That," Kratz proudly proclaimed, "is what we alchemists call *athanor*, a furnace where many of our transformations occur. Some operations require heating for as long as forty weeks." After admiring it for a few moments, Kratz became serious.

"Enough talk. Come out of this room and take the next door to your right, which is my laboratory."

Kratz kept his gun pointed at Daniel's back as he slowly exited the room and walked through the entrance into the next room. Kratz followed behind him and moved around to sit at his desk. He motioned with his pistol for Daniel to sit in a chair across from him.

"Now, would you like to hear my story? Before you die, I think you would like to know more, yes?"

"Of course," Daniel said, hoping the story would be a long one. He wondered how he was going to get out of this with his life. He had faced death twice on Rapa Nui and survived, but that was with the help of his grandfather and parents.

Kratz began, "For many years, I have been interested in alchemy, and, about twenty years ago, I had the idea for a project to produce a Philosopher's Stone. I had adequate funds from an inheritance to begin such an undertaking, but I knew I couldn't do it alone." Kratz shrugged his shoulders. "So, I gathered a group of my closest friends from Salisbury to join the cause and, together, we formulated a list of intelligentsia from other countries to ask to join us. As you know, a wide variety of occupations were chosen to give diversity in opinion and experience.

"Convincing them to relocate here was easy, for they knew that if we were able to produce a Philosopher's Stone, we would have unlimited wealth to divide among us. Until recently, we struggled mightily and did not make significant progress. For many years, we tried the safer method, the wet way. When attempt after attempt failed, we undertook the much riskier dry way, and the result was catastrophic. Two members of our team, Olga Alexeyeva and Ian Johansen, went completely insane. Of course, you know about that."

I do, thought Daniel, *thanks to Ned.*

"At the point of giving up, we had the idea of adding the sacred energy of the shiva lingam stone to our experiment, as it had been reported to assist in the creation of a Philosopher's Stone. Unfortunately, when we tried it in our investigations without success, we believed all was lost. As we thought about it, though, given the inherent spiritual nature of the bluestone and its proximity to us, we asked ourselves, *Why not try it?* We 'borrowed' a small bluestone from an excavation site in Wales, and with our first effort had partial, but not complete success.

"We then knew to have the best chance, we needed the finest of the bluestones—one from Stonehenge. Because stealing one would likely require killing of at least one guard, the group voted not to pursue that option and to look elsewhere. So, without the knowledge of my coworkers, I took matters into my own hands and pulled off the robbery with a couple of hired thugs, who I later disposed of. Unfortunately, as you know, the guard stationed there died, but what choice did I have? I couldn't wait forever as we looked for a suitable alternative."

"Why did you put the body on the Slaughter Stone?" asked Daniel.

"That was such a nice touch, don't you think? I hoped to deceive investigators and make them think I was some kind of madman killer with a warped sense of humor."

Daniel stared at Kratz and asked, "How is that a deception?"

Kratz chuckled for a moment and then growled his words, saying, "Very funny, Hawk. Soon you'll pay for your insolence.

"To finish the story, when my coworkers came to work the following day, the bluestone was in place in our laboratory, and I threatened anyone who betrayed me with expulsion and death. They weren't happy about it—concealing murder and all that—but they were finally convinced to go along with my plan. And then, *voilà*, after all those years of hard work, by just having the sacred energy of the bluestone in our lab, success came at last."

Daniel was perplexed. "Why have you been killing the other members of your group?"

"I haven't been."

"What do you mean?"

"After the initial murder of the Stonehenge guard, my gun was stolen; I have no idea who took it. Just a few days ago, I bought the weapon I am holding now."

What? thought Daniel, shocked. Then he suddenly realized: *Another killer is on the loose. Lily is at risk. Oh, God.*

Daniel stood from his chair. "Doctor Kratz—I have to go."

Doctor Kratz ordered, "Of course you won't go. Sit down, Hawk."

"But I must leave."

"You're not going anywhere. Do you have any questions before you die?"

Daniel reluctantly sat and tried to recover from the impact of what he had just heard.

After some deep breaths and thoughts on how to stall the mad doctor, Daniel asked, "What about Ned?"

Doctor Kratz sighed. "As you may have guessed, Ned was one of the members of our consortium, and, not only that, he was one of the smartest. The ideas he generated, over the course of the seventeen years he was with us, were brilliant. But then he made a fatal error in allowing himself to become involved with the wife of Jacques Girard—Elisabeth, I believe, was her name.

"As part of the original contract of our group, to avoid suspicion from the community, we agreed not to associate socially with each other or family members. If we did, the penalty was termination, so Ned had to go. He also was told, after he was axed, that if he continued to see Elisabeth, or said anything to anyone about our secret group, his life would be forfeit."

Daniel stared straight ahead. Now he knew why Ned left the names under his door: an anonymous way for him to get even.

Kratz fingered his gun and went on. "I hated what it did to Ned. Not only did he lose a potential fortune but also his love. But, we had to be firm about our contract; there was no other option."

Daniel asked, "What about Alexeyeva?"

"I had no choice but to kill her. Even though she had gone mad, as time went on she began to say things that had the potential to reveal our plans. For the same reason, I would have killed Johansen before your interview, but I didn't have quite enough time.

"Now, about Alexeyeva. On the night she died, when I was sure Mrs. Ambrose was occupied in another area of the hospital, I spiked George's tea with Valium, and, when he was asleep, I switched off the surveillance camera to Alexeyeva's hall."

Kratz added, "By the way, Hawk, I'm sure you noticed that we have high-collared straitjackets at the hospital?"

Daniel nodded. He wasn't sure he wanted to hear more.

"It was easy to unbutton and choke her to death. It was also simple to conceal the bruises left behind on her neck by re-buttoning the collar."

Daniel felt sickened, yet he said, "Weren't you worried about Mrs. Ambrose discovering how she died?"

"I wasn't concerned at all. Mrs. Ambrose hated and was disgusted by Olga Alexeyeva because of an affair Alexeyeva had with her husband. I knew she wouldn't check her very closely."

Daniel remembered the angry tone of Mrs. Ambrose's voice when he had asked to see Alexeyeva's room. Her reaction now made sense.

"What about the Chanel Number Five that I detected in the room?"

"Hawk, your powerful sense of smell is well known. Since rumor had it that you were coming to help with the investigation, I sprinkled some at the head of the bed, hoping it would throw you off track. If you were aware of Alexeyeva's fondness for men and were suspicious of foul play, you might suspect a jealous woman. I suppose I could have chosen another more inexpensive scent, but Chanel Number Five is so distinctive."

"How many others in your group are still alive?"

"Six, excluding Johansen and myself, are still working on the project. They are already wealthy beyond measure."

I have to keep him talking. "Are they still here?"

"Yes," Kratz answered, "but not for long. We are approaching the end of our endeavor."

"Who do you think the other killer is?" said Daniel.

"I have no idea, and I don't care. I've already made all the arrangements for *my* escape. Once I'm finished with you, I'll go home and return with a truck I've rented. I'll load up the gold and the Philosopher's Stone, and I'll take them to a prearranged location, close to a small rural airport. After a series of covert flights, I'll be in Switzerland, not only with all my gold, but also with the ability to create as much as I would like."

Kratz grimaced and said, "Now it's time for you to die, but before you do, would you like to see my fortune, or better yet, the Philosopher's Stone?"

Daniel nodded, still thinking of Lily and fighting his fear for her.

They stood and walked out of the office, back into the enormous hallway. Kratz moved Daniel to a place around fifteen feet in front of the safes, watching him carefully as he opened one. Daniel dared not make an attempt to escape; he would have been instantly killed.

Daniel inhaled deeply as Kratz slowly cracked open one of the enormous doors, revealing a dazzling display of sparkling gold bars, stacked evenly in rows on steel pallets up to the very top of the safe.

"In bars?" Daniel said.

Kratz smiled at Daniel's reaction. "Yes. We took the raw gold produced by the Philosopher's Stone and molded it into bars. I will need hours to load this up, but, with the help of the forklift I've rented, I should be finished well in time before the first shift of researchers arrives. Granted, I'll be taking more than my share, but since they're already set for life, I don't think they'll mind too much." Kratz paused for a moment, a look of smug satisfaction on his face.

"Now, for the *coup de grace*," Kratz said. He then walked over to the other safe, still watching Daniel closely, and began deftly twirling the dials. After a few moments, with a *snap* Kratz opened the door, revealing what looked like a large, blood-red glass crystal with jagged edges, about the size of a bowling ball, resting on a metal stand that elevated it about four feet above the safe's floor.

Daniel was astounded. *Here before me is what humankind had sought after for millennia: the Philosopher's Stone.* He could barely breathe.

The lights from the hall made the dazzling stone glimmer brightly, yet Daniel's inner senses detected more—much more. Besides the obvious physical beauty, an inner glow, a pulsating consciousness, resided within the stone.

To Daniel's surprise, the stone silently spoke to him.

I cannot stay in the presence of evil.

I must be released.

Daniel shook his head and returned to normal awareness. He muttered to Kratz, "You'll never get away with this."

"Oh, but I will. Remember, I also have superior intelligence, like the others in my group. Every variable has been considered and reconsidered, and, now—now you will die."

Kratz raised his weapon to Daniel's chest. Gunshots rang out, but not from Kratz's gun. The sound came from behind Daniel, and Kratz clutched at his chest, blood pumping from three gaping holes. At the same time, the sound of shattering echoed from the safe holding the Philosopher's Stone.

Kratz looked with disbelief at his assailant, standing behind Daniel. "No!" he screamed, as he stared at the demolished Philosopher's Stone, which, hit by a stray bullet, had exploded into shards. Then Kratz's eyes rolled back, and he collapsed to the floor. He took one final agonal breath and died.

Daniel stared at what was once the Philosopher's Stone. He wasn't sure why, but he felt a profound sense of loss.

"Well, well, Detective Fishinghawk."

Daniel heard a familiar voice from behind him.

"Aren't you at all curious about who I am?"

Daniel turned and stared incredulously.

What? Surely not! It can't be!

Chapter 32

Standing before Daniel was Emily Trueblood.

"Surprised? You should have seen the look on Lily's face before I killed her," Emily said with an evil grin. "Note or no note, I would have had to shoot her anyway."

Furious, Daniel stepped toward her.

She aimed the gun at him, an ugly scowl on her face. "Stop right there, or I'll blow your fucking head off."

Daniel froze in position, though he wanted to grab and shake her like a rag doll.

"You see, I couldn't let anyone know I was leaving the bed and breakfast that late at night, because it would have been too suspicious. Normally, Lily would not have been at work, but because the clients were so late, I had no choice but to do the deed. But now, not a soul knows you're here, and there won't be any cavalry—as you Americans say—coming to your rescue. I saved you from death just a few moments ago, but, shortly, you will die, and there's not a thing you can do about it."

Daniel was dumbfounded. All he could say was, "How... why?"

"Oh, I suppose before I kill you, I could tell you the whole sordid story."

Daniel, still disbelieving, mumbled, "Yes... do."

"You see, unknown to my husband, I was invited to join the consortium twenty years ago. I kept it a secret, because that was one of the requirements—total concealment from everyone—and that included spouses. Every one of our group was brilliant, and I'll have you know that I fit right in. I earned a degree from Oxford with honors," she said proudly.

She makes me want to puke.

Emily went on, pleased with herself. "Even all those years ago, I knew that if we were ever able to create a Philosopher's Stone, I wanted more than my allotment. After all, I deserved it. How many others in the group had to put up with such a bloody bloke for a husband?"

Daniel winced—he was quite fond of James.

"So, knowing that, early on I acted as if I were developing symptoms of obsessive-compulsive disorder, which I allowed to worsen as the years went by. Eventually, my goal was accomplished, no one took me seriously, and I was treated as a bit of a freak. In the meantime, I began preparations for this glorious moment by taking locksmith classes in London under the pretense of visiting my sister. Of course, I did visit her when there, but I became rather good at the skill of opening safes. My instructor would tell you I was the best in the class."

Daniel wanted to fold his arms and give her his unsurpassed "Are you kidding me?" look. He figured, though, now would not be the best time for that. She still had the gun and obviously knew how to use it.

"I had already made the decision that tonight I would attempt to open those safes. I don't care how impenetrable the doctor *thought* they were, I was sure I could get into them. As a backup, that's what explosives are for, and I have plenty in my car. I have already made arrangements to transport the gold to a safe location. Details you don't need to know."

Emily rambled on, boasting. "When we stole the bluestone from Stonehenge and actually produced the Philosopher's Stone, I knew it was time to act. As part of my locksmith classes, I had also learned how to break into cars. Doctor Kratz always kept his gun under his car's front seat, so it was easy to steal. When the gold began to fill everyone's safes, the first person I visited was Penny Pumpernickel. Using my locksmith skills, I picked her door, disposed of her and stole her gold.

"After that, all in our group went on alert. They had no idea whether someone from our ensemble performed the murder and robbery, or whether it was an outsider. We lost trust in each other; but, in spite of that, I was always allowed into their homes, acting as if I were there on an emergency. After all, no one had anything to fear from obsessive-compulsive Emily."

She broke into howling laughter, bending over and nearly falling on the floor.

Daniel started to make a move for Kratz's gun, which lay on the floor beside his body.

She quickly straightened up and re-aimed her weapon at him.

"Don't or I'll shoot. Sit on the floor."

Daniel reluctantly did as he was told.

Emily suddenly had a giddy grin as she looked behind Daniel. "What a happy day! It seems the doctor has left the safes open. I can take what I want. No more Philosopher's Stone, because of my errant shot, but that's okay. With what's in the safe, plus all the gold I already have, I'll be wealthy for life." She placed her left index finger on her chin and said, "Now, come to think of it, it might be best to go ahead and kill you. I have a lot of work to do. Any final questions?"

"Were you the only one who worked in the laboratory with the fermentation process?"

"Of course. Oh, every now and then others would wander in, but they always left quickly—it was that bad. I took showers at least three times a day, sometimes at the lab, trying to keep the smell off me, but there were times when I was not able to, such as before I killed Pumpernickel and Girard."

Daniel now understood. There was far more to her taking baths than just obsessive-compulsive disorder.

"How did you know where the safes of your victims were?"

Emily rolled her eyes. "Hawk, come on now. I thought you were supposed to be one of the best detectives of the lot. We worked together in this laboratory for years, and before I killed Pumpernickel and everyone's guard went up, one of our favorite topics of conversation was the concealed locations of our safes."

"Why did you steal the bottle of wine from Girard's home?"

"Are you kidding me? On our budget, the best we could afford was cheap supermarket wine, and it is like drinking bottled shit. Girard had once bragged to me about his special collection of wines, which he kept hidden under his wine cellar, so it was easy to find that night I killed him. So, one evening, unknown to my clueless husband, I sipped down the whole bottle. It was delicious, but I overdid it and vomited all night."

Pay attention to the little things, thought Daniel. *I didn't...*

Daniel had to keep her talking. "Why didn't you steal Girard's Monet?"

"What is a Monet? I may be an amazingly intelligent woman, the smartest you'll ever meet, but I don't know anything about art."

"Why did you kill Ned?"

"Why shouldn't I have? After James told me about the two names that were left behind on that paper, I knew it had to be Ned that left the note for you. He was still upset about being kicked out of the group, even though it was years ago. James told me that Ned was taking you to the mental hospital, so I tracked him down there. I never liked Ned anyway; he thought he was better than everyone else. It was a real pleasure to see the shocked look on his face when I shot him."

"How did you carry all of that gold up the stairs?"

Emily shook her head. "Haven't I explained to you how smart I am? Of course those gold bars were heavy, but that's what moving equipment is for. I found a portable device that carries loads up stairs. Besides, I've been lifting weights, can't you tell?" She grinned and flexed her right arm.

Good God, Daniel thought. *How sick is that? Keep her going...*

"How did you know I was going to Wales?"

"I knew you were traveling somewhere because you checked out of the bed and breakfast. It didn't take much for me to get your final destination out of Green's secretary, under the pretense of holding your room for you until you returned. I would have killed you at Carn Menyn had you not ducked down at the last second. How did you know?"

"I didn't."

"It doesn't matter," she said. "No more talking; it's time to kill you. I have a lot of gold to move."

"But..."

Emily pointed the gun at Daniel's head.

Suddenly, there was movement, and two strong arms grabbed her from behind and pulled her arms in back of her, the gun clanging to the floor.

Gordon Green snapped his handcuffs in place.

Emily Trueblood struggled, but to no avail.

Green beamed at Daniel.

"Chief Inspector Green—at your service."

Chapter 33

Daniel and Gordon Green loaded a still-thrashing and increasingly profane Emily Trueblood into the back seat of the British inspector's car. After she was secured, Green closed the door.

Daniel turned to him and asked, "How? I thought I was dead."

Green said, "After our conversation yesterday, I felt bloody bothered. Part of me believed you were right; yet, I thought at the same time how crazy your ideas sounded and how silly I would look in the eyes of my supervisors—and even my Salisbury colleague, Inspector DeWoody—if I dared mention your hypothesis."

"I understand. I had the same reaction, and they were my ideas."

"That said, I thought it best to keep track of you, but I had to go it alone. I sensed that you were about to make a breakthrough, which meant personal danger for you, and I didn't want you to face a crazed killer by yourself."

Daniel couldn't wait to hear more. "So what did you do?"

Green grinned. "I mimicked what you did with Doctor Kratz, when you returned to the bed and breakfast, I put a GPS underneath your car. Once I found your car, I tracked your muddy footprints to this location."

Daniel was incredulous. "How did you know what I did to Kratz's car?"

Green lifted his bushy eyebrows and said, "I followed you. I think, in most circumstances, you would have seen me, but I believe your mind was completely occupied. Besides, I'm fairly successful at not being seen when I don't want to be. Please forgive me—I did what I thought was best."

"Forgive you? Are you crazy? Because of what you did, I'm still alive. I'll be forever grateful to you."

"As I will be to you, Hawk," Green said. "We began as colleagues, and now we've become close friends."

"Agreed. With a big smile, Daniel extended his hand. "Shake on it?"

Green smiled back, reached over and they shook hands.

"Something you should know," Green added, "as I was driving here, I heard on the police scanner that Lily, the employee at the Salisbury Bed and Breakfast, was found dead, shot in the head. I assume she was a victim of Emily Trueblood."

Tears came into Daniel's eyes. He thought of the vivacious, helpful young woman, brutally robbed of her life due to the madness of greed. He could not speak.

Green, seeing his reaction, said, in a comforting tone, "Hawk, I can't think of a thing any of us could have done to have prevented her death. Thanks to you, no one else will die, and that's a great thing."

"That's little consolation," Daniel said, as he thought of Lily's bright smile.

"I know, but keep your chin up—be British—stiff upper lip and all that."

"Thanks, I'll try," Daniel said, still feeling remorseful.

"Now," Green hurriedly added, "At any minute, a veritable army of police cars will arrive. After they appear, they will cordon off the scene and investigate it. The police will want to talk with Emily Trueblood and get statements from both of us. This will not move swiftly. When we are finished, I will drive you to your car, and you will be free to return to the bed and breakfast. Later this evening, after we have had a chance to rest, we can meet and talk things over. Is that all right?"

"Yes. I would like to spend some time processing this myself first, and then I'd like to go through it hearing your perspective. Will DeWoody be able to make it?"

"I'll phone him and ask, but I believe he's stuck in a real mess in Canterbury. If he can't attend, I will fill him in on the details when he returns. He will be bloody sorry he missed all the fireworks."

"I'm sure he will be," Daniel said.

Green focused his attention on the entry to the laboratory. "Before they arrive, I need to go back inside for a moment. What is Mrs. Trueblood doing?"

Daniel glanced over his shoulder at her. "It looks like she's in a rage. Her eyes are closed, and she's flopping from side to side."

"Good. Keep an eye on her for me. Stay here."

"All right."

Green dashed inside the building. A few moments later, he returned.

"What was all that about?" asked Daniel.

"I will explain later," Green confided. "I don't have time now."

Seconds later, sirens wailed in the distance and police lights flashed their approach from the highway. Within a few minutes, the vehicles careened into the car park of the laboratory and screeched to a stop.

Daniel shoulders sagged from exhaustion when he returned to the bed and breakfast a few minutes after eight a.m. As he walked through the front door, he saw six detectives working in the entrance way. Daniel skirted around the reception area, which had been encircled with police tape.

James Trueblood was nowhere in sight. A crudely scrawled note on the reception desk read: *No breakfast today.*

One of the detectives approached him, wearing an open grey trench coat. He was tall with jet black hair, and he spoke slowly and distinctly. "Good morning Detective Fishinghawk. I am Constable Edmundson. Chief Detective Green alerted us that you would be arriving soon. May I offer you any assistance?"

"Thank you, Constable. For now, I just want to go to my room and sleep."

"Of course, sir. My men and I will continue our work here. The Chief Inspector said you have had an ordeal with this madness."

"Yes, but all will be well now."

"Certainly, sir," Constable Edmundson said, as Daniel turned and walked toward the stairs.

In the sanctuary of his room, Daniel flopped onto his back on the bed. He lay staring at the ceiling. He shook off his sadness and phoned Mahina.

"Hello?"

"Hello, my love," Daniel said. He had been deeply fearful that he would never hear Mahina's voice again. His stoic resolve melted into tears.

"Dan-iel," Mahina asked, "what is wrong?"

"I'm just glad to know . . . you are okay."

Mahina said, "I am fine, my love. And you?"

"I'm tired and sad. Murderers have killed many. One of the killers is dead, and the other is in jail."

"Your work is so challenging. My thoughts and prayers are constantly with you."

"And mine with you. I had a dream that suggested Paoa was the evil you faced. Was he?"

"Yes."

"What happened?"

"I will tell you when you return, but, for now, I can assure you that, thanks to Roberto and Spirit, Paoa will trouble us no more."

"Roberto and Spirit? Spirit . . . the *gecko*?"

"Yes," she said with the soft laugh he loved so much.

"And Tiare?" He was almost afraid to ask.

"She is still weak but gradually recovering from the Death Prayer."

"That pleases me greatly. I am eager to hear the details," Daniel said.

"Dan-iel, I so want to see you. How soon before you leave?"

"In a few days. I still have matters to finish this evening and tomorrow, and, the following day, I'll be flying home."

"I love you, my dearest," she murmured.

"I love you too."

With an enormous sense of relief, Daniel hung up his phone and closed his eyes. Just hearing Mahina's voice brought him an intense longing to once again feel her soft, beautiful body next to his.

Daniel stood and went to his closet. He opened his suitcase and pulled out a small, white envelope. He carefully reached inside it and retrieved a pressed, red hibiscus flower.

He pondered over it for a moment, breathed deeply, and then gently placed it over his heart.

Daniel slept most of the day and was finally wakened by a phone call from Green. They scheduled a meeting for an hour later, so Daniel showered quickly, dressed and walked out of his room. As Daniel stepped down the stairs, he discovered James Trueblood sitting in the dining area, shoulders slumped, his head bowed over a half-full cup of tea.

Hearing footsteps on the stairs, James glanced up and asked, "I say, Hawk, would you care to join me for a few moments?"

"I'd love to," Daniel said. He walked over to James' table and took a seat across from him. Daniel reached over and squeezed his shoulder. He had no right words to say, but finally forced out, "How are you doing?"

James looked up at Daniel, his face tearful. "Not so good. I went to the police station today to see Emily. The officer said she refused to see me."

"I'm sorry."

"Is it true what they say?" James asked. "Has my Emily been the murderer that has stalked our town—the one who killed Lily?"

Daniel wished he could have said something different, but he couldn't. "Yes. The evidence would suggest that Doctor Kratz killed the guard at Stonehenge. Emily murdered the rest."

James began to sob. "My world has . . . turned upside down. It's like I never really knew her."

"I can only imagine your shock."

"Everywhere I look, I see her face, her sweet smile, her tears and all the precious moments we shared as a couple. You know, we were married fifty years, and just last summer we had our golden anniversary." James now trembled. "I don't know what to do next."

Daniel said, "Do you have any children?"

"Yes, two daughters, both in their late forties. They live in London with their husbands. Between the two of them, I have six grandchildren, all of them adults now and on their own." James paused and wiped his eyes with a tissue. "Both of my daughters are on their way here. They are as astonished as I am."

"May I make a suggestion?" Daniel said. With James' nod he continued, "Give yourself some time to let things settle down. Perhaps have your daughters stay here with you, and, if their schedules allow, let them help you run the bed and breakfast for a few weeks. Maybe, with time, Emily's heart will soften and the three of you can visit her. Also, spend time with friends and other family members. When you've been hurt this badly, healing will take time. Do you know a counselor?"

"Yes, a man who goes to my parish church is a practicing therapist."

"Then, honor the pain you have and talk with him about it. They say that suffering eases faster when it is shared."

"I don't know if I can talk about it just yet."

Daniel nodded. "I'm confident that someday you will be able to. Be patient with yourself—your heart will know when the time is right."

"Thank you, Hawk."

Changing the subject, Daniel had a question that had been troubling him. He asked, "James, how is your sense of smell?"

James looked shocked for a second, then he answered, "When I was a child, I had a bad case of bacterial meningitis. Since that time, I can't smell a thing."

Daniel nodded, understanding at last why James never detected the smell of rotten eggs and vinegar.

"Is there anything else can I do for you?" Daniel asked.

"Yes. Pray for Emily and me."

"I'd be honored to," Daniel said, as he and James both stood and briefly embraced.

As Daniel walked away, he felt his chest tighten with emotion.

Daniel and Gordon Green met in a small private room at a local pub, where they could chat in confidence and enjoy some traditional British food and drink. Unfortunately, DeWoody had been unable to leave his assignment in Canterbury.

The walls of their room were paneled with maple-stained wood, and the smell of brewer's yeast hung heavy in the air. A stuffed deer head with large antlers hung on the opposite wall from Daniel, staring at him with dark, unfeeling eyes. Daniel would have much preferred to see this beautiful creature alive in the wilderness, and he was reminded of when he was a young boy out tracking and hunting with his grandpa in the woods east of Tahlequah, Oklahoma. They killed only for sustenance and with reverence for the life they were taking—never for a trophy. Daniel sighed and brought his mind back to the present.

Green took a swig of Landlord Pale Ale and said, "So, I understand from your report that there were two killers, the first being Doctor Kratz and the second, Emily Trueblood."

"That's correct."

Green commented, "Crikey, no wonder we were so flummoxed about this case. Who would have guessed that two different killers would use the same gun? Mix alchemy in with the equation, and you've got a real mess on your hands."

"That's for sure."

"So tell me, Hawk, how did you ever come up with the idea of alchemy being at the root of this?"

"Let's just say I was inspired. Often answers come to me in unconventional ways."

"Well, whatever your methods, however you stimulate your mind, keep it up. It's obviously working for you."

"Thanks, I will."

"Now," Green continued, "as you know, I stayed around the laboratory for awhile longer than you. Everyone who walked onto the scene was gobsmacked after seeing all that gold, and so, this case has been taken out of my hands and put into those of the higher ups at Scotland Yard. I have no idea how much gold was in that safe, but I'm sure the worth is at least into the billions of British pounds."

"Amazing!"

"We will need months to sort out all the information, but the alchemists undoubtedly knew the end of their project was approaching; most of their records on the production process are missing, probably destroyed."

Daniel said, "Perhaps that's a good thing. If somehow someone else figured out how to make an unlimited supply of gold, the world markets would spin out of control. So much for the gold standard."

"Exactly," Green said. "Anyway, the official word from the government will be that some British gold was covertly stolen some years ago, from where we won't say, and the murders revolved around protecting the secret cache. We will say that we caught the thieves before they were able to distribute it.

"Since the information about the ballistics of the weapons has been kept under wraps, no one will know about the connection between the murder at Stonehenge and the ones in Salisbury. Not a word about alchemy will be mentioned. After all, we can't have every nutcase in the world trying his hand at alchemy, especially if they knew that a bluestone was used in the process. If word got out, in no time at all, every bluestone from Stonehenge will have been stolen, and Carn Menyn would be stripped naked of anything that resembled a stone."

"Not a pretty sight," Daniel said.

"Not at all. Now, about Emily Trueblood: Since she's been arrested, she has gradually become stark-raving mad, much like Alexeyeva and Johansen, and I believe she will be declared innocent by reason of insanity. She won't be capable of saying a word to anyone about alchemy that makes any sense. Oddly enough, she may end up at the Healing Mind and Spirit Hospital.

Daniel nodded. "Entirely fitting."

"The other members of the consortium have been arrested—their names were found at the laboratory. Of course, we have confiscated their gold as well. Since they weren't directly involved in the planning of the murder of the Stonehenge night watchman—even though they did hide knowledge of it—we are prepared to offer a plea deal for reduced time in jail if they keep their mouths shut."

Daniel said, "That sounds fair."

Green added, "Shortly, the bluestone will be packed up and shipped back to Stonehenge. Everyone in the UK will be thrilled to see its return, especially the Druids, who are likely to go off their trolley."

"Crazy, right?" Daniel said.

"Hey, you're learning British," Green replied, a gleam in his eyes.

Daniel laughed out loud.

"Now, I want you to be aware that credit for breaking this case will go to you."

"That's not necessary." Daniel waved away the idea.

"Oh, but it is, especially since it's true. Besides, I've been informed by my superiors that, due to the rather incredible amount of wealth that will now be added to the British coffers, the reward will be increased to ten million British pounds. I understand that you have a worthy cause for these funds, right?"

"I do. Thank you."

"Congratulations, Hawk, you deserve it. Blimey, aren't you at all curious why I went back into the laboratory?"

With all the concluding matters they'd discussed, Green's venture into the alchemist's lair had completely slipped Daniel's mind.

"Absolutely," Daniel said.

"I went back to inspect the remains of the Philosopher's Stone. As you know, the errant gunshot from Trueblood's gun completely shattered it. But it was worse than shattered, it was pulverized, and most of the stone looked like glassy powder, as if there was some explosive material within the stone itself."

"Seriously?"

"Yes. When I was sure that there was no way they could piece it back together, I grabbed these." Green reached into his coat pocket and pulled out two pieces of blood red stone that looked like crystal spires, holding one in each palm.

Daniel caught his breath in amazement.

"Pick one," said Green. "Not many people in the world can claim that they have a piece of a Philosopher's Stone."

"Are you sure?"

"Certainly."

Daniel took his time, looked carefully from one to another and finally closed his eyes, moving his hands over them.

"This one," Daniel said, as he carefully lifted one from Green's palm.

"Very good," Green said. "I believe you have selected well. Guard it carefully, my friend."

"Oh, I will," Daniel said, still amazed at what had just happened.

As they pocketed their stones, Green said, "Do you want to leave for home tomorrow?"

"No. I have a little unfinished business to take care of. How about the day after?"

"Ace. I'll have my secretary book your flight for you. Remember, if you ever come back this way, you have a friend in England."

"And I offer you the same hospitality if you ever fly to Rapa Nui."

"Very good, mate. Safe travels."

"And to you."

As Daniel walked to his car, a flood of emotions hit him. He still couldn't believe that the killers were Doctor Kratz and Emily Trueblood.

Lily's death remained painful to him. How he wished he could have prevented it. And he couldn't imagine how much suffering James Trueblood endured; his life had been shattered.

Daniel was ready to go home, but he still had two people he needed to visit tomorrow.

Then his work here would be done.

Chapter 34

Daniel walked through the doors of the Healing Mind and Spirit Hospital with much on his mind. The events of the past few days were overwhelming in many ways, and Daniel knew it would take some time to process them. But, for now, he just wanted to be in the present moment and give it his full attention.

After greeting the receptionist, he was sent to a conference room down the hall. He sat at one end of a large, rectangular glass table, slowly sipping a cup of lukewarm tea, one prepared earlier at the Salisbury Bed and Breakfast. That morning, he was pleased to see James Trueblood and his daughters bustling around, preparing their guests' breakfasts.

In a few moments, Mrs. Ambrose walked through the door, quietly closed it and sat next to Daniel. As before, she wore her white nursing uniform. Her face appeared to be puffy from crying, and her usually pale complexion was even paler. A bruise, once again partially concealed with makeup, was on her jaw, just in front of her left ear.

She said, "Good morning, Hawk. My nursing supervisor said you wanted to have a few words with me?"

"I do."

"Before you begin, I must tell you that Mr. Johansen died last night."

"I'm sorry to hear that."

"I'm not. In his miserable condition, he had suffered greatly. Some things worse than death, don't you agree?"

"I do. I hope that, now, Mr. Johansen has at last found some measure of peace."

"As do I."

Daniel paused for a moment and said, "May I assume that you know about Doctor Kratz and Olga Alexeyeva?"

Mrs. Ambrose broke down in tears. She wiped her eyes on her sleeve and stammered out, "How could . . . I not know? I feel so . . . embarrassed and humiliated. I did not perform my duties as a good nurse would have."

"What do you mean?"

"At the minimum, I should have given her a good post mortem looking over, especially since her death was not expected. I was not thinking clearly."

At that point, she broke down and sobbed.

"There, there, Mrs. Ambrose," Daniel said, in his most consoling voice. "You are being too hard on yourself. You could have done nothing to have prevented her death."

"True, but if I had discovered the bruises on her neck when I found her, then the investigation would have started earlier."

Daniel said, "Yes, but Doctor Kratz killed no more after that, so no one else was harmed by his hand. Besides, it's completely understandable that you didn't examine her closely. You see, I am aware of the affair your husband had with her."

Mrs. Ambrose cocked her head and looked at Daniel. "It seems that everyone knew about that. It shouldn't have made a difference, especially since I was her nurse."

"In a perfect world, you're correct. But it's not a perfect world."

"But you don't understand," said Mrs. Ambrose, "I was glad she was dead."

"Your feelings were not surprising. Be easy on yourself. I've chatted with your supervisor, and she has informed me that you are a very competent nurse. Pull yourself up by your bootstraps—it's a saying we have in the States—and get on with your life. No one gets it right all the time."

"Thank you, Hawk. I'll remember that," Mrs. Ambrose said, a look of relief on her face.

Daniel nodded and said, "Good. Now, before I leave, I have a bit of advice for you. I've seen you twice now, and each time you've had a bruise on your face."

"Oh, both times were accidents."

"I see," Daniel said. "Then I'll just say that you deserve better than what you are currently experiencing. If the problem you have—the accidents—seem to have no solution, then it would be best to remove yourself from it."

Mrs. Ambrose slightly lifted her eyebrows.

"I think you know what I mean," Daniel added.

"I do. I'll consider your words."

Daniel stood to leave. "I hope you will. Best wishes."

With that, he turned and walked out of the conference room and out of the hospital. Daniel hoped to never set foot in that wretched place again.

Daniel pulled up to one of the wealthiest homes in Salisbury. He walked to the front door and knocked.

The door opened and the fragrance of Chanel N°5 almost knocked him over.

"*Bonjour, monsieur* Hawk," Madame Girard said, in a breathless voice. "I'm so happy to see you again. Please come inside."

She directed him to the living area, past the dazzling Monet. She wore a short, tight-fitting, sparkling navy-blue dress with a low-cut neckline, which prominently demonstrated her generous cleavage. The large diamond wedding ring she wore during Daniel's previous visit was conspicuously missing. She gracefully sat down on the white couch with the fluffy white cushions. Daniel sat on a chair across from the couch.

Daniel said, "Has your sister, Monique, returned to France?"

"*Oui*. She left for Nice just this morning. She had enough of the drama and wanted to return to her home for a little peace and quiet."

"I suppose you've heard the news about your husband?"

"I have. I'm sorry to learn that my husband Jacques was involved in a scheme that involved stealing gold, though at last I know why he was murdered. I'm told that one of his co-conspirators killed him in order to steal his portion. Is that true?"

"It is, and I'm happy to report that the person that killed Mr. Girard is now behind bars."

"*Bon*, I'm glad to hear it."

"What are your plans?"

"I'm going to sell my home and my husband's restaurant and move back to Paris. Things are too dull around here. I'm ready for the faster life of the city."

"I understand. Mrs. Girard—"

"Elisabeth—I prefer that you call me Elisabeth," she said, as she fluttered her eyelashes, stared at him hungrily and sensuously lay back on the couch.

"You do know I'm married," Daniel said.

"Of course I do. What does that have to do with anything?"

"It means everything to me. Mrs. Girard, would you please sit up?"

An angry look swept across her face as she sat back up. "As you wish, *Monsieur*."

"As I was about to say, I want to ask you about Ned; I am aware that you had an affair with him. You do know he was also murdered."

Mrs. Girard paled and sat speechless for a moment. She finally said, "I did know, and, yes, I had a relationship with him. But why would you question me about him?"

"There's one piece to this mystery I have yet to understand, and I was hoping you would clear it up for me."

"*Tres bien*," she said. "Then I will tell you our story. As you are aware, I am most attracted to intelligent men, and I met Ned a little over four years ago when making a tour with my husband of the pharmaceutical company where Ned was employed. They were looking for investors, and, given our wealth, we were courted by his business for a new enterprise they wished to undertake. Ned was cute, in an odd sort of way, and I was smitten, not only by his powerful intellect, but also by his innocence.

"After the visit was over, I pulled him to the side and asked if he could meet me for dinner for further discussions. I had the feeling—call it woman's intuition, if you will—that he was also interested. And so our affair began. Ned was naïve to the ways of love, but such a quick learner he was! For a year we enjoyed the most passionate lovemaking one could ever imagine."

Daniel wasn't sure he wanted to hear all of this detail. But, if it eventually gave him the answer he needed... *well*...

"Then, three years ago he said he had to break off our relationship. I was madly in love with him and told him that I would leave my husband—God rest his soul—to marry him. 'No, no,' he said. He explained that my marriage had nothing to do with it, but he couldn't disclose any more."

"I see."

"I truly loved Ned, and to see what he became in the years that followed our separation broke my heart. But I could do nothing to persuade him to come back to me. Is it true that he was killed by the same woman who murdered Jacques?"

"Yes, it appears so."

"I hope she burns in Hell for what she has done to me. She has killed not only one, but *two* men I have loved. I will never forgive her—never."

"Mrs. Girard, before I leave, may I ask you one final question?"

"Of course, *Monsieur*."

"What did Ned call you?"

Mrs. Girard's face flushed for a brief moment. Then she laughed softly and said, "Lizzie. He called me Lizzie."

Chapter 35

Daniel sat in a crowded plane as it hovered over Rapa Nui, his adopted home. Perhaps next October, it would be a good time to return again to Oklahoma, his home of origin. But, for now, all he thought about was being in Mahina's arms and seeing his dear friend Tiare, the ninety-five-year-old Rapanui shaman who had forever changed his life.

As the plane descended through the clear sky, Daniel could see the city of Hanga Roa and Rano Kau, the dormant volcano adjacent to it. In times past, he was frightened of heights, but no more.

The plane couldn't land fast enough, and it seemed an eternity before it finally hit the runway. As he walked down the air stairs, he peered closely at the crowd.

He then heard *that* voice.

"Dan-iel! Dan-iel! Over here!"

And there she was, the most beautiful woman—inside and out—in the whole wide world, his wife, Mahina.

She waved excitedly at him.

"Mahina!" he yelled as he waved back. "I'll be there in a minute!"

She blew him a kiss. "Hurry!"

Next to her stood Tiare, beaming but looking a bit frail. To her other side stood a bare-chested Roberto Ika, with the gecko Spirit perched on his shoulder.

Roberto had a crazy expression on his face and was looking nervously from side to side. On the other side of Tiare stood Alame Koreta and Jack Daldy, also waving at him.

Daniel was so anxious to see Mahina, it took all the self-control he could muster not to run over the people walking ahead of him. After he picked out his luggage and exited the secured area, he was rewarded when she leaped from the crowd into his arms.

Daniel embraced her tightly, fully enjoying the moment. Neither spoke as they breathed deeply and once again savored the feel of each other's bodies.

"Mahina, darling, I love you. I've missed you so," Daniel whispered to her.

"I love you, too." She held him tightly. "Never stay this long away from me again, please?"

"Never."

Daniel felt a nudge at his side. As he released Mahina back to her feet, he looked over and saw Tiare. He gently hugged her, "Tiare, I'm so glad to see you, especially considering what you've been through. Are you feeling stronger?"

"Much better than I was," she said, with a slight sigh.

As Daniel looked closely at her, he discovered that, even though her body showed fatigue, the light in her eyes—her soul—was as bright as ever.

Recalling their previous conversation, Daniel said, "Namaste."

"Namaste," Tiare responded, with look of recognition.

With Tiare still in Daniel's arms, Alame Koreta embraced Daniel briefly and said, "We're glad you're back, safe and sound. There's a rumor going around, for solving the crimes in England, that you've earned a huge amount of money for the Hotu Matu'a Institute."

"That's true. It's more than we expected: ten million British pounds."

"Wow!" Alame and Jack exclaimed.

"We're looking forward to hearing about your adventures," Alame said, "but, for now, our hotel duties are calling us."

"I understand," Daniel said, "Good-bye."

"Daniel," Alame said with a hint of exasperation in her voice. "Have you forgotten you are back in Rapa Nui? For good-bye, we say 'Iorana!'"

"'Iorana!" Daniel sheepishly replied as they turned away.

Daniel looked around the area. "Does anyone know where Roberto went?"

Mahina said, "I think I saw him wander outside."

Suddenly, a series of piecing screams went up, and Daniel, Mahina and Tiare rushed out of the terminal, only to discover that Roberto, with Spirit on his shoulder, was up a telephone pole, nearing the top.

Security guards hovered around the base of it, wondering what to do.

"Roberto!" Daniel yelled. "What are you doing up there?"

"It's the Ashtar Command! They've told me to get as high off the ground as I can. They need to send me a secret message—one that could save the world from destruction. The higher I get, the easier it will be for me to hear it."

Daniel yelled again, "Roberto! Ashtar just told me the message will come to you later, when you're not around so many people. Come down!"

"Okay," Roberto said, as he slowly inched his way back down the pole. When he touched ground, Daniel embraced him and whispered in his ear, "Roberto, I can never thank you enough for watching after Mahina and Tiare. I'll be forever in your debt."

"Aw," Roberto humbly said, gasping for breath, "I was glad to do it."

"And thank you, Spirit," Daniel added.

Spirit chirped and seemed to have a little smile on his face.

Roberto's eyes bulged as he asked, "Daniel, do you know about the Ashtar Command?"

"Can't say that I do."

"It's a collection of millions of spaceships that are hovering above our Earth. They come from civilizations across the universe, and they are commanded by the extraterrestrial, Ashtar. They are watching over us."

"Oh, really?"

"Yes, there are one hundred and forty-four thousand of them—they're called Eagles—an assortment of light beings, ETs and, of course, angels, who are ready to beam us up at any time into their spaceships should things get out of hand. It could happen any second, so I've got to be ready." He proudly added, "I'm Ashtar's number one guy."

"I see," Daniel said. "What happened to the Inner Earth people, the ones you told me about before I left, the ones that were going to invade?"

"Ashtar scared them off. If he hadn't been here to keep them away, Armageddon, if it ever happens, would be like a walk in the park. The Inner Earth people are still down there, waiting for their chance to attack, but it won't happen as long as Ashtar is around."

"That's a relief," Daniel said, trying to look serious.

"Oh, Roberto," Mahina said and embraced him tightly, small tears forming in the corners of her eyes. "I love you."

"I love you too," Roberto answered. "But, now I've got to get home. Ashtar will be waiting to hear from me. Goodbye."

Spirit chirped goodbye as well, and Roberto furtively scampered off.

"Let's go home," Daniel said to Mahina and Tiare.

"Let's," Mahina and Tiare agreed together.

Daniel grabbed his luggage, and, hand in hand, he and Mahina, with Tiare close behind, headed for the car. In no time at all, they would be where Daniel longed to be.

Home, sweet home.

After a long evening of food, drink and sharing their tales, Mahina helped Tiare to her bedroom. Tiare was improving, day by day, but she was still not capable of staying by herself, and Daniel was glad she remained in their home. He wouldn't want it any other way.

Mahina tended to her, and Daniel was sitting on the couch when his cell rang.

"Hello," Daniel answered.

"You ol' son-of-a-sea-cook, how you doing?"

"Kip Kelly! I'm fine, what's up with you?

"Hawk, I just got a call from Chief Inspector Gordon Green of Scotland Yard, and he told me that you've done it again. Now you're an international star, and James Bond doesn't have anything on you! He tells me that you've busted a ring of frickin' gold thieves and found enough frickin' gold to buy a foreign country. Just the thought that some of that gold might enter the market has dropped the price of gold over fifty percent. What the hell? Why didn't you tell me what you were going to do, so I could have unloaded all my positions in gold mining shares out of my retirement plan?"

"Chief, I—"

"Shit! Because of you, I'll be here with the freakin' NYPD for another fifteen, twenty more years, working my ass off trying to catch criminals and pay my bills."

"I'm sorry, chief. I had no idea."

"Hawk, it's okay—really. Truthfully, I don't know what I'd do if I didn't have this freakin' job with the NYPD, so it's probably for the best.

"Anyway, that's not the reason I called. Commissioner Walsh is about to blow a gasket to get you back. I have the feeling that, if you weren't married, just to sweeten the pot, he'd set you up on a date with his beauty queen daughter, Matilda—and she is a looker!

"Get this, though: He's now offered to pay you seven—you heard me—*seven* times what he used to pay you. He's even thrown in an extra two week vacation at his home in Nantucket Bay. Hell, he'll even let you use his yacht! How can you say no?"

Daniel didn't pause. "Chief, please tell Commissioner Walsh that I appreciate his kind offer, but I have to decline, just the same."

"Are you fargin' kidding me? You're refusing the best offer ever made in the history of the NYPD?"

"That's right."

"Hawk, you're a tough nut to crack. Commissioner Walsh will be none too happy, but I'll give him your regrets. Remember, if circumstances change, the NYPD wants you, and the offer stands, no matter how long it takes."

Daniel said, "Thanks, Chief," and then the line went dead.

Mahina returned and sat next to him on the couch.

"Who was that?"

"An old boss of mine who wants me to come back to New York."

"And?" she asked, a questioning look in her eyes.

"I told him no, as if you didn't already know."

Mahina chuckled. "You're right, I did."

"How is Tiare?"

"I know she must look bad to you, but, trust me, she is much better than she was. I anticipate she will have a full recovery. I give her healing treatments at least twice a day."

"What?"

"Something I learned in my shaman education. By the way, I need someone else to practice on," she said, pointing a finger at him. "Do you mind?"

"Not at all."

Daniel added, "So, from what you've told me, you've made great progress in your shaman training."

"Right."

"You've discovered your spirit animal—the *tavake*—you've reconnected with your parents, you've become a healer and you have helped fight off the evil shaman, Paoa."

"Yes."

"You've been very busy since I've been gone."

Mahina laughed softly and nodded.

"For a while, I felt guilty for leaving you to face an unknown evil, which you later discovered to be Paoa. Are you stronger because I was not here?"

"Yes, Dan-iel, I am."

"Then Tiare was right."

"Yes."

Mahina moved closer to Daniel. He began to feel his passions rise. He breathed slowly in and out. He observed Mahina was doing the same.

She said, "And you solved the mystery of the murders at Stonehenge and Salisbury, and have explored the ancient art of alchemy. What is alchemy again?"

Daniel explained, "Alchemy is the science of transformation. Alchemists attempt to change something that is imperfect into something purer. This could be about changing lead into gold, or even bettering the body, mind or spirit."

"That is profound." She paused for a moment, and then asked, "Now I need to know. Are you stronger because I was not there?"

As much as he hated to admit it, he answered, "Yes."

With a curious look on her face, Mahina asked, "Didn't you tell Tiare and me earlier that you were given a small piece of the Philosopher's Stone, the object that can activate the change you were talking about?"

"I did. Here, it's in my pocket. Would you like to see it?"

"I would love to."

Daniel produced the blood-red piece of the Philosopher's Stone, and he handed it to her.

Mahina held it up to the light, and splashes of red lit up the wall behind them. Mahina then placed it to her chest.

"Dan-iel," she murmured. "I feel a presence here."

"I agree. There's something about it that is mysterious and inexplicable."

Enough talk, Daniel thought. The passion he was feeling had become nearly unbearable. He took the stone from Mahina and placed it on the coffee table. He then leaned over and kissed Mahina's moist, supple lips.

She hungrily reciprocated.

Daniel stood and lifted Mahina up from the couch into his arms. He carried her into their bedroom and placed her on top of the bed. He lay beside her, and they removed each other's clothing, slowly, patiently, enjoying every second. As their ardor increased, the cool Rapa Nui breeze from their open bedroom window cooled them.

In the middle of the night, Tiare awoke from a deep sleep. She didn't feel like her old chipper self, yet she intuitively believed that she would soon be as good as new. Tiare was joyful thinking about how happy Daniel and Mahina were to see each other. It reminded her of the times she had with Ernesto, her late husband, and how delightful it was to be back with him after periods of separation.

Tiare sighed. How she wished she would have realized, at the time, that such intimate moments are limited and sacred. They do not, and cannot, go on forever. Sexuality and youth will, at some point in time, give way to the limitations of aging. And, aging will eventually yield to the specter of death. Physical separation from loved ones is not just a possibility, but an inevitability, which makes every moment—every second—of being together precious beyond measure.

Even though Tiare was aged, she still had a lot of life left in her bones. She looked forward to more growth and learning experiences. For she knew, if she stopped stretching her wings, she might as well die.

Not me, she thought. *I still have much more of life I want to taste. What would that be?*

She smiled as she thought about the possibilities. But, for now, she nestled into her pillow, blissfully bringing back her intimate moments with Ernesto. She had countless precious memories to sustain her.

And she wished for many, many more for Daniel and Mahina.

Acknowledgments

In March 2015, my wife Sheridan and I, daughter Sarah and guide Pat Shelley hiked up a gradual incline through a muddy field with scattered pools of standing water. A thin layer of high, white clouds overcast the sky as we wound our way up an unmarked trail that led to Carn Menyn, one of the sources of the mystical Stonehenge bluestones. A cultivated pine forest stood to our left, and a large, boulder-strewn hill loomed to our right.

Many more people travel to Stonehenge, and rightfully so. When we visited the ancient monument in 2013, I felt overpowered by deep transcendent feelings, some no doubt from Stonehenge itself, but perhaps others from emotions deposited by pilgrims who had visited the site during its thousands of years of existence. Any description in words remains inadequate.

But few visit Carn Menyn, and no question its remote location has something to do with that. Why would anyone in their right mind take a five and a half hour train ride from London to Wales, and then drive the narrow country roads bordered by high hedgerows, just to see a pile of allegedly holy rocks in the middle of nowhere? The Preseli Hills are gorgeous by anyone's standards, but they don't have the cachet of standing breathless before Stonehenge.

But as we trudged up the hillside, I knew that visiting this sacred place was necessary for me to complete my book in progress, *Murder at Stonehenge*. Many months beforehand, as I was putting together my writing plans, I had an "Aha!" moment when I pored over the map and saw the Preseli Hills. A striking sense of premonition cuddled me in its reassuring embrace. I was certain I was headed there and was happy for it.

Acknowledgments

After we arrived at Carn Menyn, I experienced a tranquil feeling of reverence. As our small group quietly wandered among the rocks, I thought back to the events of 2,500 BC, when the stones were first removed from this area and transported to Stonehenge. Why were certain ones selected? What is it about the bluestone, in particular, that made an ancient people want to move it over such a long distance? Questions swirled through my mind, most without answers. But, perhaps that is as it should be. Some mysteries are never meant to be revealed; rather, they remain buried beneath the rubble of time, laughing at our vain efforts to understand them.

Many deserve recognition for the construction of *Murder at Stonehenge*. I owe a huge debt of thanks to the late Georgia Lee, an Easter Island guru, who years ago assisted me during the writing of *Murder on Easter Island: A Daniel "Hawk" Fishinghawk Mystery*. She was constantly available to answer my continued questions about Easter Island, which the islanders prefer to call Rapa Nui. Her recent death has left a void that will never be filled.

Much appreciation is due my oldest daughter, Sarah, who lived in London at the time of our odysseys to Stonehenge and Wales. She helped me and Sheridan negotiate the somewhat challenging UK rail system, and while perhaps we could have made it to our destinations on our own, my suspicion is, without her help, we would have ended up in parts unknown. Sarah was also a superb travel comrade, and, as her father, I couldn't be more proud of her and her accomplishments.

I also wish to thank Dr. Gladys Lewis, a retired registered nurse and Ph.D. English professor, my primary editor for this book. She is the wife of Dr. Wilbur Lewis, a close friend of mine who became a high quadriplegic in a tragic accident some years ago. Wilbur eventually died as the result of his injuries, and his story is detailed in my book, *Oklahoma Is Where I Live: and Other Things on My Mind*. Gladys has superb editorial skills, and I will be forever grateful for her assistance.

A major contributor to *Murder at Stonehenge* was Pat Shelley of Salisbury and Stonehenge Guided Tours. Pat was the guide on our tour of Stonehenge, and later he led us on a grand adventure to Carn Menyn and other locations in the Preseli Hills. After our return home, he continued to answer my many queries, and I cannot thank him enough for his help.

Acknowledgments

Appreciation is also warranted for Lizi Trendell, a native Brit from Surrey. Her painstaking editing of my American way of putting things made the dialogue of *Murder at Stonehenge* more authentic from a British perspective.

Many thanks, once again, to Betsy Lampe of Rainbow Books, Inc. Her continued support as a publisher and editor is deeply appreciated, and her masterly contributions added a great deal to the compilation of this book.

Last, I want to express my deepest gratitude to my wife Sheridan, who was a willing and enthusiastic partner as we traveled to Stonehenge and later traversed the chilly, blustery hills of Wales. This book is dedicated to her, and for good reason. Sheridan is my best friend and traveling companion *par excellence*. I am profoundly blessed to have her in my life.

The writing of *Murder at Stonehenge* was a splendid adventure into the land of spirit. Thank you, all of my readers, for joining me on this ethereal journey. My hope is that there will be many more to come.

About the Author

Gary D. Conrad lives with his wife, Sheridan, and their dogs, Karma and Buddy, in Edmond, Oklahoma. Gary is an emergency and integrative physician, and his interests include Tibetan rights, meditation, the music of Joseph Haydn, organic gardening, choral work and wilderness hiking.

Gary is the award-winning author of *The Lhasa Trilogy*, *Oklahoma Is Where I Live: and Other Things on My Mind*, and *Murder on Easter Island: A Daniel "Hawk" Fishinghawk Mystery*. He is currently working on his experiences in emergency medicine, titled *The Pit: Memoir of an Emergency Physician*, as well as a sequel to *The Lhasa Trilogy*.

Gary can be reached through his website at GaryDConrad.com.

Printed in Great Britain
by Amazon